HOW TO BE
A YOUNG
#WRITER

OXFORD
UNIVERSITY PRESS

Oxford University Press is a department of the University of Oxford.
It furthers the University's objective of excellence in research, scholarship,
and education by publishing worldwide. Oxford is a registered trade mark of
Oxford University Press in the UK and in certain other countries

Text © Christopher Edge 2017
Database rights Oxford University Press
Illustrations © Pádhraic Mulholland 2017
The moral rights of the author and illustrator have been asserted
Folio image: secondcorner/Shutterstock.com

First published 2017

British Library Cataloguing in Publication Data
Data available
ISBN: 978-0-19-837648-4
1 3 5 7 9 10 8 6 4 2
Printed in Great Britain by Bell and Bain Ltd, Glasgow

Paper used in the production of this book is a natural,
recyclable product made from wood grown in sustainable forests.
The manufacturing process conforms to the environmental
regulations of the country of origin.

HOW TO BE
A YOUNG
#WRITER

Written by
Christopher Edge

Illustrated by
Pádhraic Mulholland

OXFORD
UNIVERSITY PRESS

CONTENTS

INTRODUCTION

Whether you're looking for inspiration to get you started as a writer or want to learn how to share your stories with the world, you'll find the advice you need in the pages of this book.

Every stage of writing a story is covered, from creating killer openings and building believable worlds to fixing plot holes and editing your final draft. This guidance will help you to understand how stories work and give you the support you need to create your own.

This book also unlocks the secrets of the writing life. From finding an agent and publisher to promoting and performing your work, you'll find hints and tips about how real writers share their stories both online and in the real world.

The world is made of stories. Whether you want to write novels, fan fiction, films, plays, TV shows, radio scripts or videogames, this book will build your confidence as a writer and stimulate your creativity.

Every writer is a reader and I hope this book inspires you to create and share your own amazing stories.

HOW TO USE THIS BOOK

This book takes you through the different stages of writing a story from finding inspiration and planning a plot to writing and editing your final draft.

If you're just starting out as a writer you can read the book from cover to cover, but if you're looking to improve a story you've already written or want to learn how to get it published, you can jump to the right section to find the advice you need.

You'll also find the following helpful features in the book.

WORD LISTS AND CHECKLISTS

Use the word lists and checklists to help you to understand the different aspects of writing a story and improve your own writing. Providing prompts and questions to help you to plan and reflect on each stage of writing a story, and vocabulary lists that you can draw on in your writing, the word lists and checklists will help you to unlock the key features of great fiction.

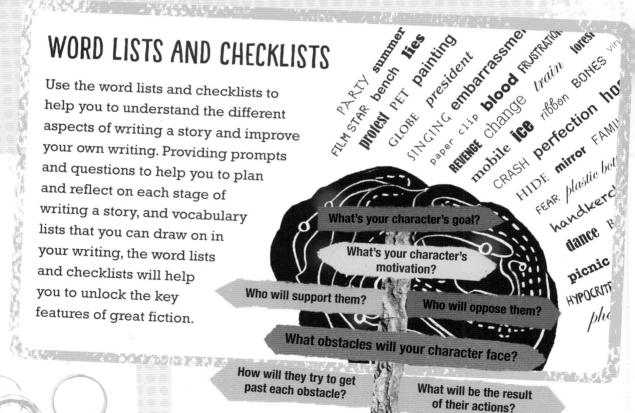

PARTY summer lies
FILM STAR bench PET painting
protest GLOBE president
SINGING embarrassment blood FRUSTRATION
paper clip REVENGE change train forest
mobile ice ribbon BONES viru
CRASH perfection FAMIL
HIDE mirror
FEAR plastic bot
handkerc
dance R
picnic
HYPOCRIT
ph

What's your character's goal?

What's your character's motivation?

Who will support them?

Who will oppose them?

What obstacles will your character face?

How will they try to get past each obstacle?

What will be the result of their actions?

How will they react to this?

AUTHOR ADVICE

With hints, tips and friendly words of encouragement, listen up for advice from some award-winning and bestselling writers.

" MARK HADDON SAYS ...

I wanted it to feel like a rollercoaster. With a turning point in the middle corresponding to the highest point of the ride where gravity takes over and you start accelerating towards the finish. "

MARK HADDON IS THE AUTHOR OF
THE CURIOUS INCIDENT OF THE DOG IN THE NIGHT TIME.

OUT OF THE BOOK

Take a look at extracts from some fabulous fiction and try out the techniques they use in your own writing.

I write this sitting in the kitchen sink. That is, my feet are in it; the rest of me is on the draining board, which I have padded with our dog's blanket and the tea cosy.
I CAPTURE THE CASTLE by Dodie Smith

'I have to go.' She leaned over so the receiver was close to the base.
'Eleanor – wait,' Park said. She could hear her dad in the kitchen and her heartbeat everywhere.
'Eleanor – wait – I love you.'
ELEANOR & PARK by Rainbow Rowell

My name is Harriet Manners, and I am a genius.
I know I'm a genius because I've just looked up the symptoms on the internet and I appear to have almost all of them.
ALL THAT GLITTERS by Holly Smale

SPOILER ALERT!

If you spot a spoiler alert, don't read the extract unless you already know what happens in the book!

BEATING THE FEAR OF THE BLANK PAGE

So you want to write a story but you don't know where to start? Perhaps you've got a dozen ideas zooming around your head but you can't find a way to get them out of your brain and onto the page. Or maybe you like the idea of writing a book but haven't got a clue of the tale you want to tell. Try some of the following tactics to get your story started.

ALL YOU NEED IS A BOOK

Look for sparks of inspiration in the books and stories that you love. Even famous writers borrow ideas and make them into their own stories.

Frank Cottrell Boyce got the idea for his book *Millions* about two brothers who find a bag of money from the 14th century story *The Pardoner's Tale* about a group of friends who find treasure.

Malorie Blackman's *Chasing the Stars* is based on Shakespeare's play *Othello*, but changes the lead character into a girl and sets the action in space!

Think about how you can give any ideas you borrow a twist to make them into your own.

" MICHÈLE ROBERTS SAYS ...

I asked myself a question whose answer I didn't know, so that writing the resulting novel or story became a voyage into the unknown.

MICHÈLE ROBERTS IS THE
AUTHOR OF FICTION AND POETRY.

BE PREPARED

You never know when inspiration will strike. Make sure you're ready by having a place to write your ideas down close to hand.

This might be a notebook or even an app on your phone.

You could babble your ideas into your voice recorder or use your camera to take a photograph of any inspirational things that you see.

Don't wait to note down your ideas – they might have disappeared by the time you get home.

" NEIL GAIMAN SAYS ...

You get ideas from daydreaming. You get ideas from being bored. You get ideas all the time. The only difference between writers and other people is we notice when we're doing it.

NEIL GAIMAN IS AN AWARD-WINNING AUTHOR OF ADULT AND CHILDREN'S FICTION. "

BE AN IDEAS COLLECTOR

Things that you find could be the starting point for a story. From a crumpled note found on the classroom floor to a piece of driftwood washed up on a beach, use these as inspiration to dream up different stories. Ask questions about the object such as

How did it get here?

Who might be looking for it?
What could it be used for?

Think about different genres of stories you like, such as horror or romance. Think about how a particular object might be used in a certain type of story. For example, a valentine's card from a secret admirer could be the start of a beautiful love story or maybe the opening of a twisted tale of terror.

NOTES

SET YOUR MIND FREE

Try 'free writing' to get your ideas flowing. This is where you write about a certain topic for a set period of time. Don't worry about your spelling, punctuation or grammar – free writing is all about unlocking your creativity.

Choose a topic from the brain-web below and write about this for five minutes. Get down on the page every thought, memory or connection this topic makes you think of – no matter how random this seems. When you look back at what you have written you might find a thought, word or phrase that sparks off a story idea.

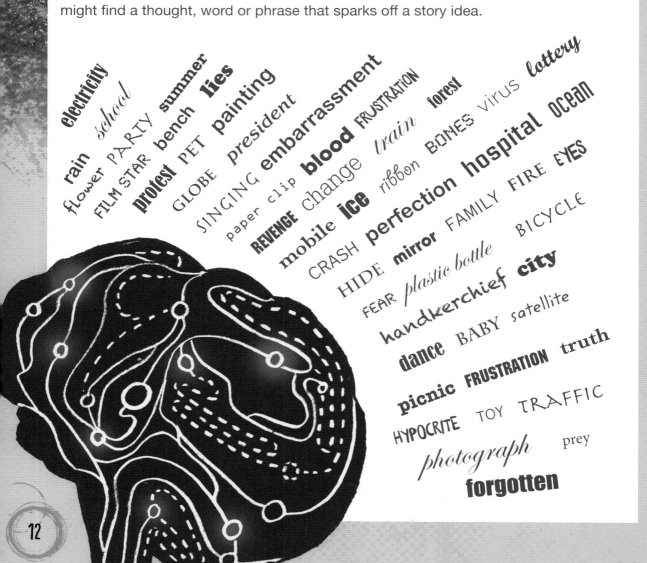

electricity
rain
school
flower PARTY summer
FILM STAR bench lies
protest PET painting
GLOBE president
SINGING embarrassment
paper clip blood FRUSTRATION
REVENGE change train forest
mobile ice ribbon BONES virus lottery
CRASH perfection hospital ocean
HIDE mirror FAMILY FIRE EYES
FEAR plastic bottle BICYCLE
handkerchief city
dance BABY satellite
picnic FRUSTRATION truth
HYPOCRITE TOY TRAFFIC
photograph prey
forgotten

MAKING CONNECTIONS

Stories don't just appear in an instant. Authors create plots by connecting different ideas, characters and settings to turn these into a story.

If you keep a note of every spark of inspiration you find, looking back at these can help you to make connections that you might not have thought of in the first place.

Don't be afraid to change any of your initial ideas as the story starts to take shape.

GET THE WRITING HABIT

Every idea for a story is just a seed. Writing regularly will help this seed turn into a complete story. If you wrote just one page of your story every day, within a few months you would find you had written enough words to fill a book.

Find a space to write. This could be anywhere from the kitchen table to the library.

J. K. Rowling famously started writing the first Harry Potter story in a cafe.

Other authors write on trains and aeroplanes.

Where you write is much less important than the fact you *are* writing.

Don't fool yourself into thinking that you always need to write in the same place. Authors can find inspiration in the strangest of places.

I write this sitting in the kitchen sink. That is, my feet are in it; the rest of me is on the draining board, which I have padded with our dog's blanket and the tea cosy. I can't say that I am really comfortable, and there is a depressing smell of carbolic soap, but this is the only part of the kitchen where there is any daylight left. And I have found that sitting in a place where you have never sat before can be inspiring. I wrote my very best poem while sitting on the hen house.
I CAPTURE THE CASTLE by Dodie Smith

THE STORY OF YOU

IT'S ALL ABOUT YOU

Every story is about someone so why not make it you? And the best person to write it, of course, has to be you! This doesn't mean that you're writing your autobiography, but taking inspiration from things that have happened to you to create fictional stories.

MEMORIES AND REFLECTIONS

Think back to your earliest memory. What is this about? Note down the details that you remember.

What can you see?

What do you hear? Can you recall any other sensations such as smells or tastes?

Think about the different emotions that this memory brings.

Being able to draw together these details in your writing can help you to create believable scenes, changing these real-life experiences into story inspiration.

PEOPLE AND PORTRAITS

Sometimes real people can find their way into the stories you want to tell. This doesn't mean that you should turn your friends and family into fictional characters, but basing a character on a real person can help you to bring that character to life for a reader.

Think about a person you know well. Note down any interesting details about the way they **look**, how they **dress**, the way they **act** and the things they **say**. Could you give any of these characteristics to a character in your story?

Maybe it could be the way they always touch their nose before they tell a lie. Or how they sometimes wear sunglasses even on a cloudy day.

Make sure you only borrow one or two details and change other things so that you create your own original character and not a carbon copy of a real person.

Taking a look in the mirror too can help you to think about the qualities your character can have both inside and outside.

Make a list of your best and worst qualities and how you show these.

Could you give any of these to the characters you create?

CHRISTOPHER EDGE SAYS ...

I think every character I write has a part of me in them.

CHRISTOPHER EDGE IS THE AUTHOR OF THE MANY WORLDS OF ALBIE BRIGHT AND THIS BOOK!

Writing a diary from the viewpoint of a fictional character can help you to explore their feelings about the different events that take place in your story.

It's hard to say exactly what it is that makes me hate school so much. It starts the moment I wake up and realize that I have to step into my bottle-green uniform. That's when it seeps away, what little confidence I have. On with the shirt … I'm slipping away … the pinafore to keep me in my place … and now the tie … to knot tight the hard lump of swallowed words swelling my throat. The day drags on … hour after hour until 3.30 p.m.
ARTICHOKE HEARTS by Sita Brahmachari

LOOKING BACK

Think about any memories these prompts could inspire. Could you use any of these as a starting point for a story?

my favourite game

my grandparents

the first time I was scared

a memorable journey

my worst day ever

moving away

friends and enemies

my favourite place

the lie

my saddest experience

in my room

the best time in my life

the first day

my first crush

an embarrassing moment

TRUTH AND LIES

Remember, you don't need to stick to the facts when you're writing fiction. Think about times in your life when you wished that things had happened differently. Maybe this is a moment when you made a mistake or something went wrong.

Imagine what would have happened if you had made a different decision. Try to write an alternative version of this moment where you put things right.

What consequences might this have?

How might your life have changed?

Thinking about actions and consequences can help you to create believable plots.

SECRETS AND CONFESSIONS

Some stories are built around secrets, so think about the following questions to create stories in a range of genres.

What could the secret be?

Who might be keeping the secret and why?

How would they feel if this secret was discovered?

You could write a paranormal romance where the heroine discovers that her boyfriend is actually a werewolf. Or a comedy about two identical twins whose friends keep on mixing up their secrets with hilarious consequences.

DIARIES AND BLOGS

Writing a diary or blog can help you to work through your feelings about the things that happen to you. These could inform the stories that you write, inspiring characters, plots and settings. Asking **What if** and **If only** questions can help to transform the facts of your life in to fiction.

RESEARCHING YOUR STORY

When you've got the idea for your story don't rush into writing it straight away. Whether this is an epic science fiction tale about an interstellar mission to save humanity or a historical comedy about Henry VIII's dating disasters, there's bound to be some information you need to find out first.

ASKING THE RIGHT QUESTIONS

Make a list of questions about your story that you need to find the answers to. These might be questions about the setting, the characters or any aspect of the plot.

If you're writing a detective story about a murder investigation you might want to find out how evidence is collected at a crime scene nowadays. But if your story is set in Victorian times, you'll need to discover what kinds of evidence police looked for at the time.

Did you know that fingerprint evidence was only used in English courts for the first time in 1902?

Getting the facts right will add to the believability of your story.

FRANCES HARDINGE SAYS ...

It's necessary to make people real. Characters may be motivated by love, power, whatever it is, but they need to eat, sleep and shelter.

FRANCES HARDINGE IS THE AUTHOR OF *THE LIE TREE*.

RESEARCH TOOLS

When you know what you want to find out, it's time to start your research. From reference books to online searches there are lots of tools you can use. You could start by looking at a broad topic such as 'superstitions' and then narrowing down your research to focus on a particular aspect or question that is relevant to your story, e.g. 'Why is Friday 13th seen as unlucky?'

One of the best places to research your story is the library. Libraries are filled with inspirational stories and librarians can help you to find the right books for your research.

Explain what you want to find out and why.

Don't be afraid though to change the focus of your research if you discover a new fact or interesting piece of information that might send your plot in a different direction.

The information you find in a book is often more reliable than information you find online, so when using the Internet for research always try to find more than one source for the facts you find out.

When searching online, use quotation marks around words and phrases to narrow down your results and the minus sign in front of any terms you don't want included.

Keep a note of the information you discover and where you have found this.

You may find it helpful to bookmark useful websites so you can find these again quickly.

RESEARCHING CHARACTERS, SETTINGS AND PLOTS

Think about the characters, setting and plot of your story. Use these questions to help you decide the areas you need to research.

CHARACTERS

- What do I need to find out about my characters?
- Do my characters have any special skills I need to research?
- Are there any real-life models for the characters in my story that I could find out more about?

Setting

- Where does my story take place?
- Can I base a fictional setting on a real-life location?
- Are there any real-life locations I can visit or research online?
- What do I need to find out about the setting?

Plot

- What facts do I need to find out to make my story believable?
- Does my plot require any expert research?
- Who do I need to talk to?

With a library it is easier to hope for serendipity than to look for a precise answer.
WHEN DID YOU SEE HER LAST?
by Lemony Snicket

'Google' is not a synonym for 'research'.
THE LOST SYMBOL by Dan Brown

EXPERT ADVICE

Sometimes you can't find the facts you need online or in a book. Maybe you're plotting a dystopian story about a killer virus and need some in-depth medical advice. Asking an expert can help you to find out more detailed information and ensure that you don't make any mistakes.

Professional organizations linked to the topic you are researching can often help with expert advice, so if you're writing a science fiction story about a comet crashing into the Earth, contacting an astronomy society could help you find out the facts you need.

Using social media to post questions can be a quick way of getting a response.

Remember though to make sure that you protect yourself online when using the Internet to contact people and organizations.

GETTING SWAMPED

Don't let your research take over your story. Sometimes it can feel like there's just one more fact you need to find out, but this might just be your brain's way of stopping you from starting your story! You can always find out more information as you write, so at some point you need to put your research to one side and start writing chapter one.

Too much information can be just as intimidating as too little. After you have collected your research, go through it to find the essential information that will help you to write your story. You could organize your research into different folders linked to key scenes, settings or characters from the story. This will help you to easily find the information you need at the right time.

PLOTTING AND PLANNING

If you look up the word 'plot' in a dictionary, you will find several definitions. The most important definition for this book is the one that says that plot is 'the story in a play, novel or film'. It's the events that happen in the story and the sequence these are presented in.

However, a definition of the verb 'plot' is 'to make a secret plan'.

When you're turning your initial story idea into a plot, it can helpful to plan what's going to happen before you start writing it.

Other authors prefer to make up the story as they go along, seeing where their characters take them.

Whichever method you choose, thinking about the plot can help you to create a great story. Look at your favourite books and films and think about how their plots work.

TOP SECRET

plot *noun*
the story in a play, novel or film

PLOT
STORY
ENDINGS
RESOLUTION
PROBLEMS
CHALLENGES
BUILD-UP
BEGINNINGS

conflict *noun*
a fight, struggle or disagreement

BUILDING YOUR PLOT

Think about the starting point for your story. What happens in your opening scene?

Which characters are involved?
What are they doing?
What happens to them?

Why? Asking questions about this scene will trigger ideas about what happens next. You can use **spider diagrams**, **charts** and other note-making techniques to record your ideas.

One way to organize your ideas into a coherent plot is to create a **story mountain** or **ladder**. This is where each event or action in your story builds on the one before. As your story moves forward you want to build up the drama. Each action contains the seeds for the next event.

Think about the conflicts your main character might face. What's stopping them from jumping straight to the top of the story mountain to achieve their goal?

Planning the obstacles you will put in your character's path and thinking about how these link together will help you to create an effective plot.

23

THINKING ABOUT YOUR PLOT

Use these prompts to help you to think about the plot of your story.

What's your character's goal?

What's your character's motivation?

Who will support them?

Who will oppose them?

What obstacles will your character face?

How will they try to get past each obstacle?

What will be the result of their actions?

How will they react to this?

What is the cause and effect of each key event in your story?

What questions will be answered?

What new questions will arise?

What complications might there be?

How can you raise the stakes to build tension and excitement?

Do things happen to your character or does your character make things happen?

" MARK HADDON SAYS ...

I wanted *Curious Incident* to grip readers on the first page and hold their attention to the last. I wanted it to feel like a rollercoaster. With a turning point in the middle corresponding to the highest point of the ride where gravity takes over and you start accelerating towards the finish. "

MARK HADDON IS THE BESTSELLING AUTHOR OF *THE CURIOUS INCIDENT OF THE DOG IN THE NIGHT-TIME*.

CLIMAX AND RESOLUTION

Some authors know the very last scenes of the story from the moment they write the opening lines. Other writers discover the ending only when they get there. Whichever way you write, you need to make sure that your narrative reaches a climax.

In a detective story this might be the moment where the murderer is unmasked, or in a fantasy adventure, the final confrontation between the hero and their deadliest enemy. This is the moment of the greatest drama which the story has been building to.

After the climax comes the resolution. This is where you tie up any loose ends and how your main character has been changed by the events of the story. You don't have to make this a happy ending, but it should leave your readers feeling satisfied when they read the closing line.

VISUALIZE

Use a graph or flow chart to plot the action of your story. This can help you to think about how different events link together. Or create a table listing the names of the key characters in your story and plotting the scenes they appear in. Don't be afraid to change your plan if a better idea occurs to you when you're writing your story.

AVOIDING PLOT HOLES

A plot hole is something that stops your story making sense.

There might be a moment in your story where your hero sprains her ankle but then starts sprinting in the very next scene.

Or maybe a character who's been lost in the desert for days suddenly answers a call on their mobile phone!

Make sure that there are logical links between the events of your story. If your characters start acting in a way that doesn't make sense or something happens for no good reason, this should get your plot hole detector buzzing.

CAROLINE LAWRENCE SAYS ...

Plot is what happens in your story. Every story needs structure, just as everybody needs a skeleton. It is how you 'flesh out and clothe' your structure that makes each story unique.

CAROLINE LAWRENCE IS THE AUTHOR OF **THE ROMAN MYSTERIES** SERIES.

Where you begin your story can influence the way you construct your plot. Read the opening of Donna Tartt's novel and think about how the plot could develop from here. Might it continue with the search for Bunny's killers or go back in time to tell the story of how he died?

The snow in the mountains was melting and Bunny had been dead for several weeks before we came to understand the gravity of our situation. He'd been dead for ten days before they found him, you know. It was one of the biggest manhunts in Vermont history – state troopers, the FBI, even an army helicopter; the college closed, the dye factory in Hampden shut down, people coming from New Hampshire, upstate New York, as far away as Boston.
THE SECRET HISTORY by Donna Tartt

MAKING CHARACTERS REAL

Think about the stories that you love. From Harry Potter to Sherlock Holmes, Scout Finch to Katniss Everdeen, the pages of great books are filled with unforgettable characters. A story isn't just a sequence of events – it's how characters make things happen and react to the things that happen to them that turns a plot into a story.

You need to believe in the characters in a story in order to care about what happens to them. This doesn't mean your readers have to *like* your characters. If you filled your story with perfect heroes and heroines, it wouldn't seem very realistic. Make your characters real by giving them flaws and failings, just like real people.

MOTIVE AND CONFLICT

The main character in a story is called the protagonist. Think about the protagonist in the story you want to tell.

Why do they act in the way they do?

What do they want?

What do they need?

Don't force your protagonist to fit into a pre-determined plot, but let your plot grow out of your protagonist's motives.

Your protagonist's actions and desires can fuel the conflict in the story.

Who wants to stop them from achieving their goal?

An antagonist is a character or group of characters who might stand in your protagonist's way. Remember you need to give your antagonist their own motives to add to the believability of your story. Conflict between characters can often come when they share the same goal or have opposing goals.

CHANGE IS GOOD

Don't treat the characters you create as dolls or puppets on a stage. Think of them as real people and consider how they will develop over the course of the story. The plot can be a journey of discovery for your protagonist, where they make discoveries, find out things about themselves and are changed by their experiences.

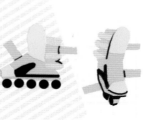

CHARACTER PROFILES

Use these prompts to create character profiles for your protagonists, antagonists and the other key characters in your story.

Manner of speaking
(e.g. softly spoken, sarcastic, pompous, etc.)

DISTINGUISHING FEATURES

Physical characteristics
(e.g. height, build, hair colour, etc.)

Habits/ mannerisms

Character name

STRENGTHS

What this character needs

What this character wants

Favourite sayings

HOW DO THEY FEEL ON THE INSIDE?

How do they act on the outside?

What this character fears

WHAT MOTIVATES THIS CHARACTER?

WEAKNESSES

HOW DO OTHERS VIEW THIS CHARACTER?

How will this character change?

GETTING INSIDE YOUR CHARACTER'S HEAD

The characters you create shouldn't be surface deep. Just as in real life, what the reader sees on the outside may not always reflect how the character feels on the inside. As an author you can share the character's thoughts and emotions with the reader if you wish, but also show these in the way you describe your character's actions and decisions.

MAGGIE STIEFVATER SAYS ...

That's how I create my characters. I start out with a real human model, then I strip it away so it becomes someone who's even better, and then I finally come up with a character who's someone only I could write. But they all start out with a human heart.

MAGGIE STIEFVATER IS AN AUTHOR OF YOUNG ADULT FICTION.

If you're writing a crime story, think carefully about the motivation of your protagonist.

If you make this character a grizzled police detective, they've got a ready-made reason for investigating crime.

But if you want to make your protagonist a teenage girl, you need to think of a good reason why they would want to solve the crime that kicks off the story.

Maybe their younger brother goes missing and they were the last person to see them alive?

Make your characters more believable by showing *why* they do the things they do.

motivation *noun*
a reason for a person to do something

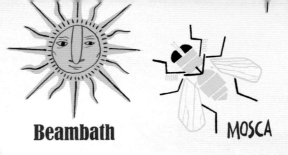

Beambath

MOSCA

You can use dialogue to reveal your characters' hopes and desires.

'Damn, damn, damn,' she said.
'I never said why I like you, and now I have to go.'
'That's okay,' he said.
'It's because you're kind,' she said.
'And because you get all my jokes ...'
'Okay.' He laughed.
'And you're smarter than I am.'
'I am not.'
'And you look like a protagonist.'
She was talking as fast as she could think. 'You look like the person who wins in the end. You're so pretty, and so good. You have magic eyes,' she whispered. 'And you make me feel like a cannibal.'
'You're crazy.'
'I have to go.' She leaned over so the receiver was close to the base.
'Eleanor – wait,' Park said. She could hear her dad in the kitchen and her heartbeat everywhere.
'Eleanor – wait – I love you.'
ELEANOR & PARK
by Rainbow Rowell

NAMING YOUR CHARACTERS

The names you give your characters can influence how your readers respond to them. If you're writing a fantasy tale about a brave warrior who battles dragons your reader probably won't believe in your story if you call your protagonist 'Steve'!

The names you choose can reflect the qualities you give your characters. Books and websites of baby names often include information about the origin of the name and what it originally meant.

Why not choose the name 'Kadir' which means 'powerful' for the name of your warrior, and 'Alden' which means 'old friend' for your hero's faithful companion.

If you're writing a story set in the past, refer to historical sources to find out which names were commonly used at the time.

If your story is set today, take a look at a newspaper to help you pick out a character name.

J. K. ROWLING SAYS ...

I love inventing names, but I also collect unusual names, so that I can look through my notebook and choose one that suits a new character.

J. K. ROWLING IS THE AUTHOR OF THE HARRY POTTER SERIES.

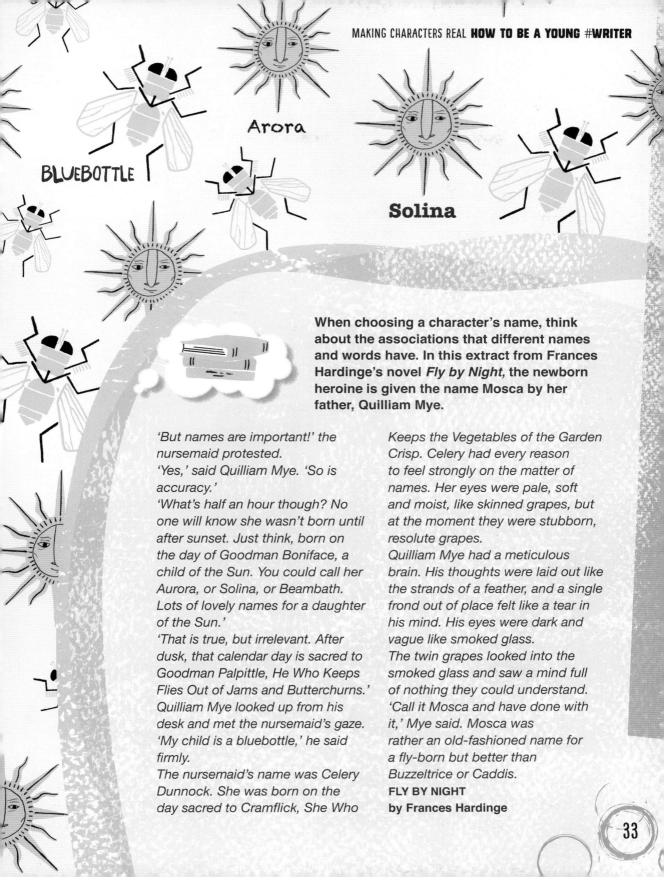

Arora

BLUEBOTTLE

Solina

When choosing a character's name, think about the associations that different names and words have. In this extract from Frances Hardinge's novel *Fly by Night*, the newborn heroine is given the name Mosca by her father, Quilliam Mye.

'But names are important!' the nursemaid protested.

'Yes,' said Quilliam Mye. 'So is accuracy.'

'What's half an hour though? No one will know she wasn't born until after sunset. Just think, born on the day of Goodman Boniface, a child of the Sun. You could call her Aurora, or Solina, or Beambath. Lots of lovely names for a daughter of the Sun.'

'That is true, but irrelevant. After dusk, that calendar day is sacred to Goodman Palpittle, He Who Keeps Flies Out of Jams and Butterchurns.' Quilliam Mye looked up from his desk and met the nursemaid's gaze. 'My child is a bluebottle,' he said firmly.

The nursemaid's name was Celery Dunnock. She was born on the day sacred to Cramflick, She Who Keeps the Vegetables of the Garden Crisp. Celery had every reason to feel strongly on the matter of names. Her eyes were pale, soft and moist, like skinned grapes, but at the moment they were stubborn, resolute grapes.

Quilliam Mye had a meticulous brain. His thoughts were laid out like the strands of a feather, and a single frond out of place felt like a tear in his mind. His eyes were dark and vague like smoked glass.

The twin grapes looked into the smoked glass and saw a mind full of nothing they could understand.

'Call it Mosca and have done with it,' Mye said. Mosca was rather an old-fashioned name for a fly-born but better than Buzzeltrice or Caddis.

FLY BY NIGHT
by Frances Hardinge

BUILDING YOUR WORLD

When your reader steps into the pages of your story, you want them to believe in the world that you've created. This means you need to think as hard about the details you leave off the page as those you include on it.

DRAWING A MAP

If you're writing a fantasy story, you might want to **draw a map** to help you to visualize the geography of the strange lands you are inventing. This is what J. R. R. Tolkien did before he wrote *The Hobbit*, with his maps of Middle-Earth filled with mountains, rivers and forests, giving him ideas for new scenes and even new stories as the world of Middle-Earth grew.

MAKING HISTORY

Think about the history of your world.

What events have happened to create the setting the reader encounters on page one?

If you're writing a futuristic dystopia like *The Hunger Games* where characters are forced to fight to the death, asking questions such as 'Why is life like this?' will help you to create a more believable world.

KEEPING IT REAL

Even if your story is set in a time and place your reader will recognize, you still need to think about the details you include to make the world on the page a perfect mirror to the real world. Be careful though not to include too many references to the latest pop star or must-have gadget as these might date your story for future readers.

VISUALIZE YOUR WORLD!

Use the words below to help you to visualize the world of your story. What ideas do the different words suggest? Think about how they could fit into your story.

Remember to consider the consequences of the decisions you make. How might the choices you make affect the lives of your characters? For example, if your story is set in a world where everyone has magical powers, what laws might there be to govern how these are used?

LANDSCAPE GEOGRAPHY language SUBTERRANEAN gothic etiquette communication Victorian magical fashion urban mega-structures diseases education FUTURISTIC ALIEN EXOTIC TECHNOLOGY RAW MATERIALS renaissance BELIEFS ANIMALS STEAMPUNK SLUMS utopian MOUNTAINOUS tools families weapons ancient MEDIEVAL dystopian energy desolate lunar CRIME TECHNOLOGICAL history environment city state government BUILDINGS friendships commerce PRIMITIVE SOCIAL PROBLEMS architecture contemporary WASTELAND CIVILIZATIONS industrial travel transport behaviour law historical

INSPIRATION

If you're struggling to find inspiration, take a look on Pinterest or use other online tools to help you find images of the people and places that could populate your story.

What kind of clothes do your characters wear?

What does the place they live in look like?

Create a **mood board** that gathers together pictures, quotations and other inspirational materials that help you to imagine the world of your story.

JEFF NORTON SAYS ...

Whatever story you're writing, it's crucial to carefully construct the world that the characters inhabit — it'll lead to a richer, more fully realized story; one that the reader/viewer will want to relish and revisit.

JEFF NORTON IS AN AUTHOR, WRITER-PRODUCER AND FOUNDER OF *AWESOME*.

ROOM FOR IMAGINATION

Don't think that you need to know everything about the world before you begin writing your story. Remember you're writing fiction not a history book! Focus on the aspects of the world that are important for the story you want to tell and leave some blank spaces for the reader to fill with their imagination.

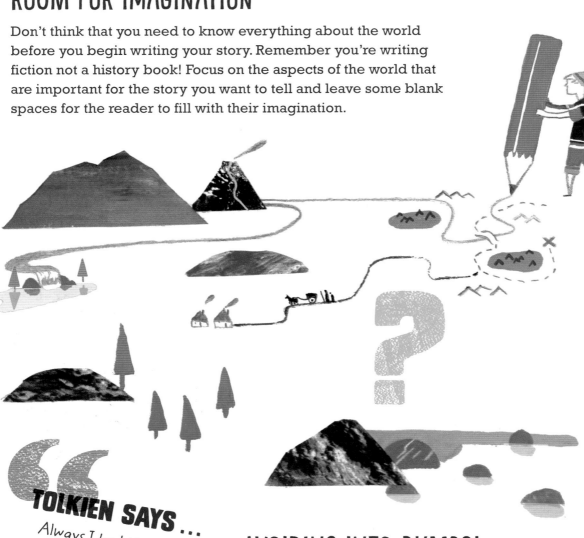

TOLKIEN SAYS ...

Always I had the sense of recording what was already 'there', somewhere: not of inventing.

J.R.R. TOLKIEN WAS AN ENGLISH WRITER AND POET, WHO IS BEST KNOWN AS THE AUTHOR OF THE CLASSIC HIGH-FANTASY WORKS **THE HOBBIT, THE LORD OF THE RINGS** AND **THE SILMARILLION.**

AVOIDING INFO-DUMPS!

When you're writing, use action and dialogue to drop in details about the world, but avoid the dreaded info-dump! This is where you bury the reader under an avalanche of facts and forget that you're telling a story. The world-building that you've done should enrich your story, not take it over.

M. JOHN HARRISON SAYS ...

Every moment of a science fiction story must represent the triumph of writing over world-building.

M. JOHN HARRISON IS A SCIENCE FICTION AUTHOR.

LAINI TAYLOR SAYS ...

I think with world building, it's important to create a sense of culture even if it is a fantasy.

LAINI TAYLOR IS THE AUTHOR OF THE *DAUGHTER OF SMOKE AND BONE* SERIES.

Read these extracts and think about what you learn about the worlds where they're set.

This was the home of people from the other side. The mystery isn't what happened to them, it's how they found themselves on the wrong side of The Wall in the first place.
THE WALL by William Sutcliffe

The island of Gont, a single mountain that lifts its peak a mile above the storm-racked Northeast Sea, is a land famous for wizards.
A WIZARD OF EARTHSEA by Ursula Le Guin

'No interruptions, boy!' Alby shouted. 'Whacker, if we told you everything, you'd die on the spot, right after you klunked your pants. Baggers'd drag you off, and you ain't no good to us then, are ya?'
THE MAZE RUNNER by James Dashner

CHOOSING A VIEWPOINT

Before you begin to write your story, you've got an important decision to make.

How do you want to tell your story?

The point of view you choose will influence the details you include and also how your readers respond to the story.

WHOSE STORY IS IT ANYWAY?

Think about the plot of your story. Who would you say the main character is? This will be the person who is driving the plot of the story forward as things happen to them and they react to these events.

If you're writing a thriller, this might be a spy who uncovers a plot to assassinate the Prime Minister, but then has to go on the run as she's framed for the same crime.

If you can clearly identify a single protagonist in your story, this will be the perspective you want to tell the story from.

FIRST-PERSON VIEWPOINT

Imagine this character holding a video camera to create a film of the story as you write it. Every scene is seen through their eyes and the reader can share their thoughts and emotions as the story twists and turns.

If you're writing a horror story about a visit to a haunted house, writing in the first person can ramp up the suspense as the narrator can't know what's around the next corner ...

The main disadvantage of choosing to write from a first-person perspective is that it limits the information you can share with the reader. You can describe a scene only if your narrator is there. This might stop you from writing a story where you need the reader to know a key piece of information before the protagonist.

GETTING INSIDE THE MIND OF YOUR NARRATOR

When you are writing in the first person you need to take on the persona of your narrator. As you write, use these questions to help you to think about every scene of the story from their point of view.

How is the narrator feeling at the start of this scene? Why?

What important information does the narrator know at the beginning of the scene?

What important information does the narrator not know at this point?

What does the narrator think is going to happen in this scene?

What does the narrator want to happen in this scene?

What might surprise the narrator in this scene?

What emotions will the narrator feel and why?

Which other characters will the narrator encounter in this scene?

What are the narrator's feelings towards these characters?

What will the narrator think about the events of the scene?

How does the narrator feel at the end of the scene?

ME, MYSELF AND I

If there is more than one main character in your story you can still use a first-person viewpoint.

If you are writing a love story like *Romeo and Juliet* you might want to tell the story from both points of view, switching chapters to let each character tell their version of the story.

Or how about a thriller about a bank robbery that's gone wrong? You could tell the story of the robbery from the viewpoint of different characters in the gang.

Switching between different first-person perspectives in a single story can be tricky to pull off and sometimes confusing for readers. Make sure that it's the right decision for your story and you've got the confidence you can make it work before you try it.

LANCE RUBIN SAYS ...

I've always loved a first-person narrator. It makes me feel like I'm hanging out with my most uninhibited friend. And if this friend is funny, I'm even more likely to keep reading.

LANCE RUBIN IS AN AUTHOR OF YOUNG ADULT FICTION.

In Tom Ellen and Lucy Ivison's novel *Never Evers*, the two main characters Mouse and Jack tell the story in alternating chapters. Each chapter starts with the name of either Mouse or Jack to make it clear to the reader who is telling the story.

Mouse
'You can't stay in there for ever.'
I rolled my eyes dramatically even though she couldn't see me and climbed into the bath fully clothed. I lay down and crossed my arms like a snoozing vampire. And then a bottle of Herbal Essences fell on my head.
I did realize that living in the bathroom was not a long-term life plan. It was a last-chance-saloon act of desperation. At some point I was going to have to either jump out of the window, or just unlock the door and skulk back out. Not exactly Braveheart material. I wonder if anyone has ever locked themselves in a bathroom and come out victorious?

Jack
The three of us were sat smack bang in the middle of the coach, where we always sat on school trips. This was our natural position. Where we belonged. We're not geeky enough to sit right up front, near the teachers, but we're also definitely not cool enough to be mucking about at the back with the football players and the psychos. We're middle-of-the-coach material, through and through.
NEVER EVERS by Tom Ellen and Lucy Iveson

PHILIP PULLMAN SAYS ...

I write almost always in the third person, and I don't think the narrator is male or female anyway. They're both, and young and old, and wise and silly, and sceptical and credulous, and innocent and experienced, all at once. Narrators are not even human — they're sprites.

PHILIP PULLMAN IS THE AUTHOR OF
HIS DARK MATERIALS.

THIRD-PERSON VIEWPOINT

When you write from the third-person viewpoint, you use a narrator to tell the story, not one of the story characters. You should use third-person pronouns such as 'he', 'she', 'it' or 'they' to tell the story. However there is more than one type of third-person viewpoint – third-person limited or third-person omniscient – so think carefully about which would be the best way to tell your story.

THIRD-PERSON LIMITED

Using the third-person limited means that the narrator tells the story from the point of view of one character. Most fiction is written in this style and it is usually the main character's viewpoint. The reader can share the character's thoughts and feelings so it is similar to the first person but, because the narrator can dip in and out, it can also give more distance from the main protagonist.

THIRD-PERSON OMNISCIENT

If you are 'omniscient' you know everything. When writing from a third-person omniscient viewpoint the reader can share every character's perspective. Rather than a single camera showing the events of a scene, the reader can switch between multiple cameras, each equipped with a mind-reading microphone to pick up on different characters' thoughts and feelings.

The morning after noted child prodigy Colin Singleton graduated from high school and got dumped for the nineteenth time by a girl named Katherine, he took a bath. Colin had always preferred baths; one of his general policies in life was never to do anything standing up that could just as easily be done lying down. He climbed into the tub as soon as the water got hot, and he sat and watched with a curiously blank look on his face as the water overtook him. The water inched up his legs, which were crossed and folded into the tub. He did recognize, albeit faintly, that he was too long, and too big, for this bathtub – he looked like a mostly grown person playing at being a kid.
AN ABUNDANCE OF KATHERINES by John Green

FINDING YOUR VOICE

Whether you use the first person or the third person to tell your story, you are using a narrative voice. If you write a story from the first person's viewpoint, your protagonist's character will need to shine through.

If your narrator is a nine-year-old schoolboy think about the words and phrases he would use to describe events and express his emotions.

You wouldn't expect this character to describe a crowded playground as a 'throng of students' or talk about feeling 'overwrought' instead of excited.

Choose vocabulary that reflects your narrator's age, background and knowledge.

The narrative voice you create can also communicate your narrator's attitude to people, places and things.

If they describe their teacher as 'boring' you can tell that the narrator isn't very interested in what their teacher has to say!

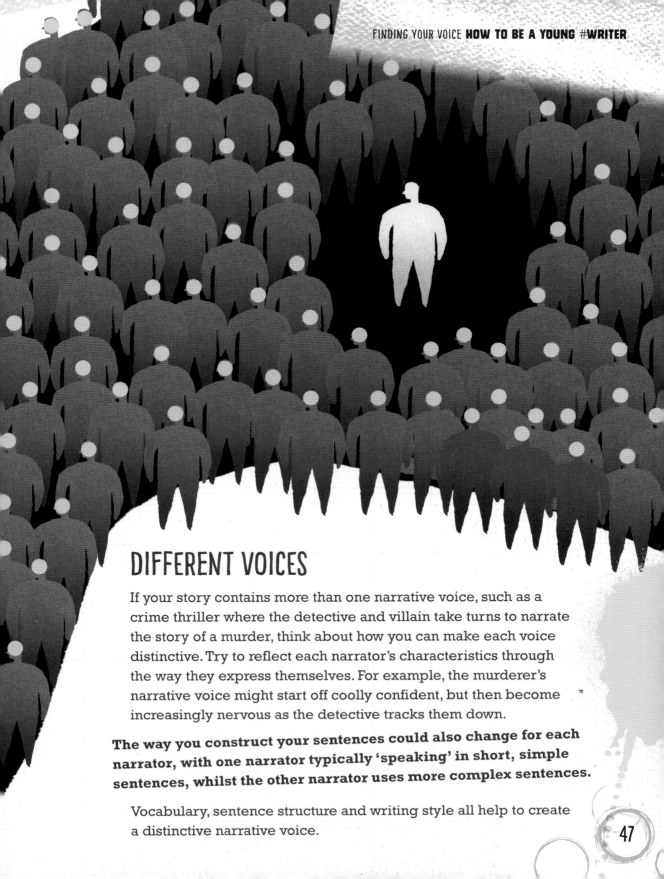

DIFFERENT VOICES

If your story contains more than one narrative voice, such as a crime thriller where the detective and villain take turns to narrate the story of a murder, think about how you can make each voice distinctive. Try to reflect each narrator's characteristics through the way they express themselves. For example, the murderer's narrative voice might start off coolly confident, but then become increasingly nervous as the detective tracks them down.

The way you construct your sentences could also change for each narrator, with one narrator typically 'speaking' in short, simple sentences, whilst the other narrator uses more complex sentences.

Vocabulary, sentence structure and writing style all help to create a distinctive narrative voice.

47

GETTING THE TONE RIGHT

The tone of voice you choose for your narrator can change as they respond to the events of the story. Look at the world of the story through your narrator's eyes to help you capture their voice.

sympathetic
excited
SINISTER
resentful smart
SCARED embarrassed
SARCASTIC
INTELLIGENT
cautious
cheerful
dreary
brave
kind
DULL
calm
jolly
EAGER
gentle

ANNOYED
obnoxious quizzical
irritated HURTFUL
COURAGEOUS
romantic fresh
secretive
MOODY
MYSTERIOUS
happy
SMUG
angry
clever
sad
silly
bold
foolish
grumpy

AUTHORIAL VOICE

If you choose to tell your story from a third-person viewpoint, there is still a narrative voice that tells the story. However rather than this voice belonging to a character, this is sometimes called the authorial voice. This is the distinctive style of writing that the author has chosen to tell a particular story.

Sometimes authorial voice can be informed by the particular genre that the story belongs too.

If you're writing an action story you might write in short sentences and use language that helps to create a tough tone of voice.

If you are writing a funny story you might regularly use parentheses that include comic asides to add humour to the story being told.

Look at novels from the genre you want to write in to see how different authorial voices are created.

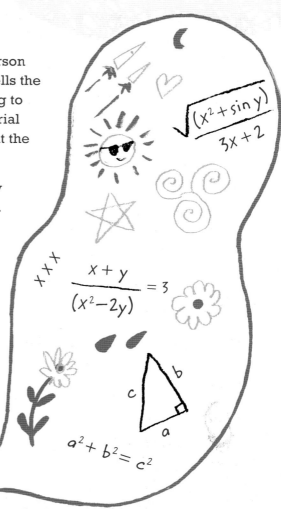

$$\sqrt{\frac{(x^2 + \sin y)}{3x + 2}}$$

$$\frac{x + y}{(x^2 - 2y)} = 3$$

$$a^2 + b^2 = c^2$$

CHRISTOPHER EDGE SAYS ...

If you're writing a first-person narrative, think about the character who is telling the story. Do the words you are choosing sound as if they belong to this character? Sometimes reading your writing out loud can help you to capture and maintain a convincing narrative voice.

CHRISTOPHER EDGE IS THE AUTHOR OF
THE MANY WORLDS OF ALBIE BRIGHT
AND THIS BOOK!

Look at the different narrative voices created in these extracts. What impression do you get of each narrator?

My name is Harriet Manners, and I am a genius.

I know I'm a genius because I've just looked up the symptoms on the internet and I appear to have almost all of them.

Sociological studies have shown that the hallmarks of extraordinary intelligence include enjoying pointless pursuits, an unusual memory for things nobody else finds interesting and total social ineptitude.

I don't want to sound big-headed, but last night I alphabetised every soup can in the kitchen, taught myself to pick up pencils with my toes and learnt that chickens can see daylight 45 minutes before humans can.

And people don't tend to like me very much.

So I think I've pretty much nailed this.

ALL THAT GLITTERS by Holly Smale

Miss Connolly, our old teacher, always said start your story at the beginning. Make it a clean window for us to see through. Though I don't really think that's what she meant. No one, not even Miss Connolly, dares write about what we see through that smeared glass. Best not to look out. If you have to, then best to keep quiet. I would never be so daft as to write this down, not on paper.

Even if I could, I couldn't.

You see, I can't spell my own name.

Standish Treadwell.

Can't read, can't write,

Standish Treadwell isn't bright.

MAGGOT MOON by Sally Gardner

EXPERIMENTING WITH VOICE

You might not find the right voice to tell your story straight away. Maybe you've written the first chapter from a third-person viewpoint, but then got stuck because something about this doesn't feel right. Try choosing a character and rewriting the chapter from their perspective.

How does this change the feel of your story?

Remember your narrator doesn't have to be the main protagonist. In Arthur Conan Doyle's *Sherlock Holmes* stories, he often uses Dr Watson to narrate Holmes' adventures. Writing **letters**, **emails** and **blogs** from your narrator's viewpoint can help you to capture their voice. You could even include some of these in your story.

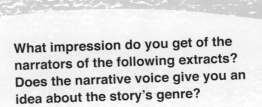

What impression do you get of the narrators of the following extracts? Does the narrative voice give you an idea about the story's genre?

As far as the world is concerned, I am good. When I am with my father – as he receives his councillors or the ambassadors from foreign courts – I hold my tongue. I contrive to look intelligent. They flick their eyes to me, they look for something – anything – to interpret. But I say not a word. My face is framed for obedience. They cannot know my thoughts.
VIII by H. M. Castor

The walk back to the toilets gave me the chance to think about the Shank's threat. It was bad. It was really bad. I was like a cow with a cut leg in the Amazon river, just waiting for the first piranha to get a sniff of the blood.
HELLO DARKNESS
by Anthony McGowan

WEAVING DESCRIPTION INTO YOUR STORY

It takes two people to make a story: the author who writes the words on the page and the reader who brings them to life in their mind. As you write, think carefully about the way you describe each scene of your story. In fiction the most effective description brings together character, setting and action in a way that moves the story forward.

IT'S ALL ABOUT THE DETAILS

Try to identify the key details that will bring each scene to life. These might be details that are essential to the plot of your story, such as mentioning a knife that your central character is using to chop vegetables that at the end of the scene will become a murder weapon.

The details you choose can be a short cut for your reader to quickly get a sense of character and place. A well-chosen detail can help you to suggest the mood and atmosphere of the scene.

From a raised eyebrow to communicate a character's disbelief to the creak of a cot in an empty nursery, the details you include can amuse, chill or surprise your reader, influencing the way they respond to a scene.

Don't overload your reader with unnecessary details, just focus on the ones that help to tell your story.

STEPHEN KING SAYS ...

Description begins in the writer's imagination, but should finish in the reader's.

STEPHEN KING IS AN AUTHOR OF HORROR, FANTASY AND SUPERNATURAL FICTION.

WEAVING DESCRIPTION INTO YOUR STORY

WEAVING DESCRIPTION INTO YOUR STORY

MEG ROSOFF SAYS ...

When you read a book, the neurons in your brain fire overtime, deciding what the characters are wearing, how they're standing, and what it feels like the first time they kiss. No one shows you. The words make suggestions. Your brain paints the pictures.

MEG ROSOFF IS AN AUTHOR OF YOUNG ADULT FICTION.

A NEW SENSATION

Put the reader in touch with your characters' experiences by appealing to their senses. From sights and sounds to the sensations of touch, taste and smell, use the words below to help your reader to experience the events you're describing.

BARKING BLARING **buzzing**
chattering *chiming* chirping clanging
CLINKING **croaking** CRACKING DRIPPING FIZZING
grating GURGLING HISSING **jangling moaning**
rasping rattling scratching SNARLING **thudding**
WARBLING **jarring** PIERCING rasping
RAUCOUS SHRILL THIN
tinny

acrid bitter **crisp**
earthy fresh mildewed
musky **musty** *oily* pungent *sharp*
rancid sour stagnant *fragrant*
scented **stinking** ODOROUS **reeking**
ROTTEN fetid FOUL NAUSEATING
ACIDIC **burnt fiery** fruity
metallic *zesty*

Bumpy coarse *curved*
DAZZLING **dulled**
GLIMMERING **flattened**
IRIDESCENT
translucent VAST MINUTE,
POCK-MARKED SMOOTH
fragile impenetrable

abrasive clammy DOWNY DRIPPING, GREASY
bristly FLUFFY **coarse** CREAMY CRINKLY DRY **feathery**
watery fine grainy *hairy* moist papery *rough*
rubbery RUNNY **silky** SMOOTH **soft** CRUNCHY
spongy LUMPY SQUASHY STICKY **stringy springy**
fibrous velvety **woolly**

DESCRIBING CHARACTER

Try to influence the way the reader 'sees' the characters you create by including evocative details. This doesn't just mean including details about how they look physically, but conveying their actions and emotions through the words you use to describe them.

The order in which you present descriptive details to the reader will influence the image they create.

If you're writing a science fiction story about an astronaut meeting an alien life form, don't spend nearly an entire paragraph describing the alien's crystal-blue eyes then drop in the fact that it has eight tentacles at the end!

This would totally transform the image the reader has started to create in their mind, so build up your description by focusing on the most obvious details first.

DESCRIBING SETTING

Think about the place where the scene is set. If this is somewhere that your reader will easily recognize such as a park or a playground, think about the details that will make this setting come alive. Perhaps the playground is rundown with a swing dangling from a broken chain.

Include details that help to create a specific picture in your reader's mind rather than a general image of a typical place.

If you are describing a place which will be unfamiliar to your reader, such as a historical setting or a fantasy world, you will need to describe the scene in greater detail to help your reader to visualize it. Using an authentic detail such as the unpleasant smell of a flickering tallow candle could bring the setting of a medieval castle to life for the reader.

The descriptive details you include help to convey a sense of character and setting. How do you think the character of Montgomery Flinch is feeling in the first extract? Which details give you this impression? What kind of setting is described in the second extract? Which details help you to visualize this?

Montgomery Flinch gripped the sides of the reading lectern, his knuckles whitening as he stared out into the darkness of the auditorium. His bristling eyebrows arched and the gleam of his dark eyes seemed to dart across the faces of each audience member in turn. A mesmerised silence hung over the stage; it was as if the theatre itself was holding its breath as it waited for the conclusion to his latest spine-chilling tale. The expectant hush seemed to deepen as Flinch finally began to speak.
TWELVE MINUTES TO MIDNIGHT by Christopher Edge

Frodo and Sam gazed out in mingled loathing and wonder on this hateful land. Between them and the smoking mountain, and about it north and south, all seemed ruinous and dead, a desert burned and choked. They wondered how the Lord of this realm maintained and fed his slaves and his armies. Yet armies he had. As far as their eyes could reach, along the skirts of the Morgai and away southward there were camps, some of tents, some ordered like small towns.
THE RETURN OF THE KING by J. R. R. Tolkien

DIRECTING THE READER

Don't think of yourself as the author of the story, imagine you're the director instead. Every scene of a film is made up of different camera shots from close-ups to the view through a wide-angle lens. Think about how you can use description to direct your reader's attention in a similar way.

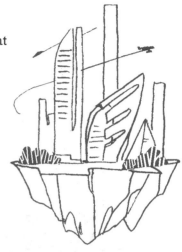

A close-up shot could be the description of a single telling detail such as a murder suspect's trembling hand.

You could use a wide-angle lens to soar above the streets of a floating city as you describe its fantastical architecture.

Think about how you move the camera's focus to guide the reader's eye as you write each scene.

If you're writing from a first-person viewpoint, the reader will experience each scene from your narrator's perspective. Think about where this character's focus will be.

What will they notice?

What's most interesting or important to them?

Describing the scene through the narrator's eyes will allow you to show their attitude to the people, places and things they encounter, so think carefully about the vocabulary you choose.

Remember, if you've introduced a character or setting earlier in the story, you don't necessarily need to spend as much time describing this again as the reader will already have a picture in their mind. However, things can change and you might focus your reader's attention on another detail to help build on or change the way they visualize this person or place.

ACTION AND CONSEQUENCE

When you think about the action of a story, your imagination might conjure up car chases, fight scenes and huge explosions. However the action of a story is anything that moves the plot forward, from a quiet event such as the accidental discovery of a ring in a romance to the kidnapping of the President's daughter in a tense thriller. Wherever there is conflict and change in your story, that's where you'll find the action.

KEEPING IT REAL

The key to writing effective action is to make sure the reader cares about the characters involved.

If you're dangling your hero off the edge of a cliff, you want the reader to gasp, not yawn, as the villain stamps on his fingers.

The reader should feel as though they are sharing the characters' experiences.

Think about how the characters involved will act and react as the action unfolds. Don't suddenly give your teenage hero superhuman powers just to get them out of a tight spot.

You need to stay true to the characters so that the reader can believe in the action you write.

Too many miraculous escapes will leave your reader feeling cheated.

Real-life research can help you to create convincing action scenes.

If you want to know what an explosion in space would look and sound like, don't watch *Star Wars* but ask a scientist instead.

In the vacuum of space any explosion would be silent, starting with a brilliant flash but without the smoke and flames you'd see here on Earth as there's no atmosphere to feed them.

ACTION VERBS

The verbs you choose can influence the way your reader visualizes the action. Think about the different pictures the verbs 'scamper' and 'scramble' create in your mind. Choose the verb that best fits the action you are describing. Remember to use the past or present tense form of the verb, depending on how you've chosen to tell your story.

hurdle SKIP **ascend** HURL SHOOT slam sprint AMBLE MAUL

lurch BOWL **zoom** file STALK **march** **propel** outstrip **streak**

zip **kick** file STALK **propel** bash STRIDE

pelt VAULT **sock** RAM slog LIMP bash STRIDE hobble

LUNGE VOLLEY **scowl** CAST SLING dawdle **tread**

pitch JUMP **dash** loft fire GLOWER **tread**

shuffle flick TROT **smash** PUNCH

FLY **dart walk** grimace BOUND boot **cosh**

stamp CLUMP **launch** heave smite

leap grin snarl wallop HIT

smack STEP **throw**

ACCELERATE **discharge** smirk

clear SPRING sneer

CHARGE **clock**

" URSULA LE GUIN SAYS ...

I want the story to have a rhythm that keeps moving forward. Because that's the whole point of telling a story. You're on a journey — you're going from here to there. It's got to move. Even if the rhythm is very complicated and subtle, that's what's going to carry the reader. "

URSULA LE GUIN IS THE AUTHOR OF
THE TALES OF EARTHSEA.

CONTROLLING THE PACE

Every author wants to write a page-turning book, but the way you write it can influence how quickly your reader turns the pages. Your story might start with a dramatic event and then keep on pumping up the action until the story ends in a crescendo, but this might leave your reader breathless.

It can be more effective to balance high-octane action scenes with slower scenes focusing on dialogue and description to give your reader a chance to recover.

If you want to increase the narrative pace, experiment with the length of your sentences and paragraphs.

Short simple sentences can create a sense of quick-fire action.

Longer sentences can slow the reader down as they layer on the detail.

Try reading your sentences out loud to see what sounds right.

61

Sometimes a character can commentate on the action as it unfolds. This can work in stories told from both first-person and third-person viewpoints. Using this technique make the reader feel as though they're sharing the characters' reactions in real-time.

I grabbed the biggest book I could and smacked him round the head with it. Neil grunted and his eyes scrunched up in surprised pain.

I swung the book at him again. It made a heavy thudding sound as it bounced off the side of his skull. He staggered backwards, holding his head in both hands. I barged into the tall shelves and slammed them with all my weight. And the whole bookcase wobbled, then tipped, then fell. All those massive books came tumbling out as the shelves pitched forward. Neil yelped as the books hit him. But the bookcase itself was even heavier.
THE RETURN OF JOHNNY KEMP by Keith Gray

Alex didn't dare look behind him, but he felt the train as it reached the mouth of the tunnel and plunged into it, travelling at one hundred and five miles per hour. A shock wave hammered into them. The train was punching the air out of its way, filling the space with solid steel. The horse understood the danger and burst forward with new speed, its hooves flying over the sleepers in great strides. Ahead of them the tunnel mouth opened up but Alex knew, with a sickening sense of despair, that they weren't going to make it.
POINT BLANC by Anthony Horowitz

SHOW, DON'T TELL

What's more exciting? Sitting in a front-row seat at the cinema to watch the latest Hollywood blockbuster, or being told what happened in the film by a friend in a cafe afterwards? When you write your story you want to give the reader a front-row seat so they can experience the action first-hand.

Try to include details that suggest or reveal rather than telling this directly to the reader.

Think about the difference between 'Sophie curled her fingers into a fist, digging her nails into her palm even as she kept a smile on her face' and 'Sophie tried to hide her frustration'. The first sentence shows whilst the second one tells. If you've chosen the right details, your reader will be able to see a character's emotions through their actions without your having to explain how they're feeling.

AVOID CLICHÉ

From screeching tyres in a car chase to a hero who walks through an explosion without a scratch, it's easy for action scenes to fall into cliché. Try to think of new ways to describe the action of your story to keep your reader interested.

Unusual or unexpected similes and metaphors can help a reader to picture a scene in a unique way.

How about describing an explosion scattering debris like dandelion seeds?

JOE CRAIG SAYS ...

Every single line of every fight or chase should tell the story. If it doesn't, an action sequence will feel kinetic but stagnant. Do not mistake movement for action. Do not mistake motion for emotion.

JOE CRAIG IS THE AUTHOR OF THE JIMMY COATES SERIES.

SCENES AND TRANSITIONS

A story is made up of moments. When authors write they want to create scenes that linger in the reader's mind long after they've put down the book. From the Battle of the Five Armies in *The Hobbit* to Lyra and Will's final parting at the end of *The Amber Spyglass*, these pivotal events move the plot of the story forward and add to its drama.

STRUCTURING YOUR SCENES

When you plan, break the plot down into different scenes. Think about how these link together. Remember you don't need to show your reader every moment in time, but can skip forward and back to focus on the moments that matter.

Every scene should have a purpose. Maybe something happens that sends the plot in a different direction or a twist reveals that a particular character is not what they seem …

Think carefully about the way you sequence your scenes. If you're writing a spy thriller or a gripping mystery you'll need scenes that help to lay clues or build tension before the action explodes in a heart-stopping climax. Don't be afraid to juggle and re-order scenes to give the story maximum impact.

START LATE, GET OUT EARLY

This doesn't mean you should only write your story when it's past midnight or knock off after writing a single paragraph. 'Starting late' means beginning each scene as far into the action as possible. If you're writing a scene where the hero arrives at a haunted house, don't waste space describing how they park their car! Think about the focus of the scene and cut straight to the action. This way the reader won't get bored with unnecessary details.

As soon as the key action is on the page, that's the signal to end the scene.

Don't try to pad out the action by describing every single detail of your character's reactions.

Cut straight to the next scene to keep up the pace of your story.

Try to end every scene with a narrative hook.

This might be a snappy piece of dialogue or an unexpected twist that that will make the reader turn the page.

ARGHHHHH!

CHANGE OF SCENE

When there is a change of time, place or character's point of view, you need to start a new scene. At the start of this new scene, it's important to quickly show the reader what has changed, e.g. indicating the new time, place or point of view. Think about how you could use or adapt some of the following phrases to do this.

'TWO HOURS LATER ...'

'NEARBY ...'

'TONIGHT ...'

'Waterloo station, rush hour ...'

'9 a.m. Monday morning, the coast was clear ...'

'After some time, the scenery changed ...'

'Only a few hours earlier the sun had been shining, now rain dripped ...'

'Now it was autumn ...'

'ONLY A WEEK LATER ...'

'Later ...'

'In the afternoon ...'

'Ross raced across the city ...'

'At first each day seemed just the same ...'

'THE SKY WAS OVERCAST ...'

'On-board the train ...'

'ABOVE THE CLOUDS ...'

'DOWN BY THE CLIFFS ...'

'In the years that followed ...'

'LATE SEPTEMBER ...'

" LAINI TAYLOR SAYS …

Never sit staring at a blank page or screen. If you find yourself stuck, write. Write about the scene you're trying to write. Writing about is easier than writing, and chances are, it will give you your way in.

LAINI TAYLOR IS THE AUTHOR OF THE YOUNG ADULT SERIES **DAUGHTER OF SMOKE AND BONE**.

Look at how the following writers quickly orientate the reader to show them where and when a scene is set.

In the bus on the way to school next morning we passed 4 red cars in a row which meant that it was a Good Day.
THE CURIOUS INCIDENT OF THE DOG IN THE NIGHT-TIME
by Mark Haddon

Now, in late September, the whiff of woody decay filled the air and the squelchy carpet of leaves gave off a heady malty smell.
THE PRISONER
by James Riordan

A hundred miles ahead, the sunrise shone on Circle Park, the elegant loop of lawns and flower-beds that encircled Tier One.
MORTAL ENGINES
by Philip Reeve

At earliest dawn our camp was astir and an hour later we had started upon our memorable expedition.
THE LOST WORLD
by Sir Arthur Conan Doyle

CHAPTER BREAKS

Some writers like to begin a
new chapter every time they
start a new scene. This can be
an effective approach if you're
writing a thriller or adventure
story as short, punchy chapters
can increase the pace of
your story.

If there is a change of scene
within a chapter, this is usually
shown on the page by a blank line.
When you're writing and want to show that
a new scene has started, insert the symbol '***'
to show where this blank line should be put.

" DAN BROWN SAYS . . .

I often will write a scene from three
different points of view to find out
which has the most tension and which
way I'm able to conceal the information
I'm trying to conceal. And that is,
at the end of the day, what writing
suspense is all about.

DAN BROWN IS THE BESTSELLING AUTHOR
OF *THE DA VINCI CODE*. "

NARRATIVE JUMPS AND SCENE TRANSITIONS

Switches in viewpoint, movement forward and backwards in time and shifts in location are all different kinds of narrative jumps that writers can use in their fiction. The key to keeping in control of those narrative jumps is to make sure your reader doesn't get lost.

Use scene transitions to signal the jump that's taken place. A scene transition might be as short as a couple of words to signal a change in time, 'Later on …' or you might write a whole paragraph to describe a new location or character. Focus the reader's attention on the key information that will help them to understand where they are in the story.

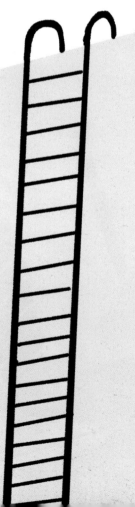

FLASHBACKS

From fiction to film, flashback is a technique where the narrative shifts to an earlier part of the story. This can be when a character's memory is suddenly triggered and a new scene recounts this earlier event that they've been reminded of.

Any flashback scene should be vital to the plot of the story. The memories we keep are those which are most important to us and that's what a flashback needs to be. Try to keep it brief and to make the scene vivid and powerful to keep the reader's attention. You can show the move to a flashback by shifting tense. Don't overuse this technique or your reader will end up confused.

WRITING DYNAMIC DIALOGUE

When characters speak stories come alive. Through their use of dialogue, authors can drive the plot forward, transforming two-dimensional characters into people who feel real as they talk about the ideas, emotions and action of the story.

LET'S TALK

The key to writing good dialogue is to make it sound natural. This doesn't mean writing the kind of speech that you hear every day. When you listen to people talk in real life, they repeat things and miss out words, put pauses in places and stumble over sentences. However, in fiction you need to edit out these features and concentrate on capturing the essence of what each character says.

Natural conversation flows so try to mimic this. Most people don't speak in full sentences or wait patiently for the other person to stop speaking before they have their say. Dialogue can overlap with one character interrupting or finishing another's sentences.

TONE OF VOICE

Dialogue can reveal a character's thoughts and emotions. Authors can show their state of mind not only through what a character says, but how they say it. As you write, try to hear a character's tone of voice in your mind.

For instance, if you're writing crime fiction think about the tone of voice a detective might use to interrogate a suspect. **Will they be aggressive or sound sympathetic to try and trick the suspect into a confession?**

You can use verbs such as 'snarled' and 'sighed' to show the way a character is speaking, as well as adverbs such as 'softly' and 'angrily', but it can be more effective to show how a character is feeling through the words they use. As you write each line of dialogue, think about the emotions of the character at this point in the story. What do they want? How do they feel? The line, 'I'm fine' can take on a different meaning if it is spoken by a character with a tear in their eye.

CHRISTOPHER EDGE SAYS ...

I often read dialogue out loud as this helps me to spot any clunky words or phrases that don't seem to ring true for the character who is speaking.

CHRISTOPHER EDGE IS THE AUTHOR OF **THE MANY WORLDS OF ALBIE BRIGHT** AND THIS BOOK!

DIALOGUE TAGS

When reading dialogue, readers need to know which character is speaking. Using a pronoun or the character's name followed by a verb such as 'said', 'asked' or 'replied' can give this information quickly and simply, e.g. 'He said' or 'Alex replied'. Other verbs and adverbs like those shown below can also be used to give more information about the way a character is speaking, but these 'tell' rather than 'show' this, e.g. *'I'm fine,' she replied sadly.* Avoid these if you can and try to communicate this information through the character's actions or dialogue, e.g. *'I'm fine,' she replied, brushing a tear from her eye.*

ADMITTED AGREED **answered** **argued** asked barked begged began bellowed BLUSTERED **bragged** CRIED **demanded** GIGGLED **hissed** HOWLED iNTERRUPTED LAUGHED **lied** **mumbled** muttered nagged pleaded promised questioned REPLIED **retorted** ROARED **sang** SCREAMED **screeched** SHOUTED SIGHED SNARLED SOBBED **threatened** **wailed** warned **whimpered** *whined* whispered wondered YELLED **petulantly** ANGRILY **sadly** CHEERILY faintly QUIETLY SOOTHINGLY LOUDLY **wistfully** **happily** quickly swiftly *gratefully* suggestively coldly CASUALLY **dolefully** DESPERATELY **anxiously** AWKWARDLY **calmly** CAUTIOUSLY CARELESSLY DELIBERATELY **eagerly** **enthusiastically** fondly gently *hurriedly* kindly mysteriously NERVOUSLY **politely** SHYLY **reluctantly**

MORDOR NEEDS YOU

ACTION AND DIALOGUE

Too much dialogue without any action can make a story read like a radio play. Writers use description to break up the dialogue, indicating a character's actions as they speak. This body language can give the reader important clues about the character's thoughts and feelings. If a character tugs at their sleeve as they speak this could indicate their nervousness or even excitement. Body language can be used to emphasize or contradict the truth of what a character says.

Real life doesn't stop to give you time for a chat and neither should the action of your story. Interweave dialogue with descriptions of what's happening to keep up the pace of the plot. If a bomb explodes in the middle of a scene, a single line of dialogue such as 'What the … ' can show the protagonist's surprise and heighten the tension.

Look at how this writer interweaves dialogue, action and description to suggest different characters' emotions.

'Granny?' I stare at her in disbelief. But yes, I know it's her now, even though I haven't seen her since I was four.

She looks at me as if I'm the one who's behaving oddly.

'Of course. Who else would I be? Now enough of this nonsense. Shall we go in?'

'No,' I say. She looks at me.

'Pardon?'

'You can't. It's Mum's house. She wouldn't want you here. You're not welcome.'

She smiles at me as if I'm still the four-year-old I was last time she saw me. 'Don't be silly, Pearl.'

'I mean it,' I say. 'Dad's not going to be too happy if he comes back and finds you've just turned up out of the blue.'

She looks at me, her plucked and pencilled eyebrows arched with surprise. 'Pearl, dear,' she says. 'Who do you think asked me to come? Did he not tell you?'
THE YEAR OF THE RAT
by Clare Furniss

73

CAPTURING CHARACTER

The way people speak in real life reflects who they are and the same is true for fictional characters too.
A character's background – where they were born, where they went to school, the job they do – all influence the way a writer presents their voice on the page. From slang and dialect phrases to the words they choose all give the reader clues about a character.

Think about the different ways you can express an idea and choose the one that best fits a particular character. In a situation where your lead character has their arm trapped beneath a boulder, a surgeon might comment, 'For the patient to survive, I will have to perform a transradial amputation', whilst a passing lumberjack would say, 'I'm gonna have to chop it off!'.

When writing dialogue, authors put inverted commas or speech marks around the words spoken. Punctuation marks should go inside these speech marks too, whilst dialogue tags can be used to break up sentences or placed at the end. In dialogue, ellipsis can be used to show hesitation or a trailing off in speech, whilst a dash at the end of a dialogue line can indicate an interruption.

'The shadow of Mordor lies on distant lands,' answered Aragorn. 'Saruman has fallen under it. Rohan is beset.'
THE FELLOWSHIP OF THE RING by J. R. R. Tolkien

'I couldn't ...' he said. Stumbling over the words. Everything changed after your dad died. Mark changed. He was like a stranger. I didn't know what to do. I didn't know what to say to him.'
BONE JACK by Sara Crowe

'What you do here?' His voice was foreign and his Ws came out like Vs.

'I ... nothing.' I could hardly spit out the words.

'Who with you?'

'No one ... honest.'
CHASING THE DARK by Sam Hepburn

'Is this a bad time?' Mum asked. 'I can call back. I wasn't sure – '

'No – it's fine,' I said. 'I just – '

'Do you need me to call back? This is a bad time, isn't it?'
MY SECOND LIFE by Faye Bird

'You should smile more often. It suits you.' She tilted her head. 'What makes Anthony so sad?'

He changed the subject.

'Where's Eve?'
HATE by Alan Gibbons

DON CALAME SAYS ...

Each character's voice should be easily recognisable. To that end, give your characters verbal tics, or words and phrases that they only use, or grammatical errors that are specific to them. Perhaps they speak in sentence fragments. Or run-on sentences. Do they overuse their large vocabulary? Do they use colorful language to get their point across?

DON CALAME IS A SCREENWRITER AND AUTHOR OF THE SWIM THE FLY TRILOGY AND DAN VERSUS NATURE.

CREATING A KILLER OPENING

You only get one chance to start a story so you need to make it count. The scene you choose needs to be the perfect introduction to the world of your story.

SETTING, CHARACTER AND CONFLICT

From dystopian thrillers that drop the reader slap-bang in the middle of the action to quirky love stories that set up an unforgettable narrative voice, a story's genre can influence the way an author chooses to begin a book.

The three key elements that are part of every opening are setting, character and conflict. Different types of story will balance these elements in different ways.

In the opening to the fantasy epic *The Hobbit*, the author, J. R. R. Tolkien, begins with a detailed description of the setting and the protagonist, Bilbo Baggins, before introducing conflict with the arrival of Gandalf.

In contrast, the historical thriller, *Constable & Toop* by Gareth P. Jones, focuses first on conflict by beginning with the grisly murder of a minor character and doesn't even introduce the protagonist until the next chapter.

WHERE DO I BEGIN?

Not every story starts at the beginning. Some writers choose to open with an event from near the end of the plot and then flashback with the rest of the story showing how the plot reached this point. Other stories begin just before the beginning, setting up the protagonist's ordinary life or everyday world before introducing the event that triggers the plot.

Wherever a writer chooses to begin, they still need to make sure that this opening scene contains enough drama. If you want to introduce characters and setting, show these in action to stop the reader feeling as though they're looking at a static photograph. The pace of an opening scene needs to carry your reader to the point where the story takes off.

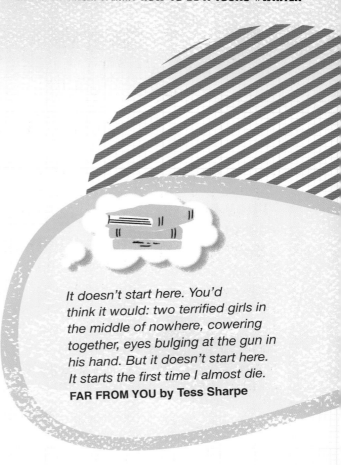

It doesn't start here. You'd think it would: two terrified girls in the middle of nowhere, cowering together, eyes bulging at the gun in his hand. But it doesn't start here. It starts the first time I almost die.
FAR FROM YOU by Tess Sharpe

FAMOUS FIRST LINES

Some readers give up on books before they even finish the first paragraph, so writers have to work hard to hook their readers' attention from the very opening line. Which of these famous first lines would keep you reading?

The early summer sky was the color of cat vomit.

UGLIES by Scott Westerfeld

They say that just before you die your whole life flashes before your eyes, but that's not how it happened for me.

BEFORE I FALL by Lauren Oliver

I had just come to accept that my life would be ordinary when extraordinary things began to happen.

MISS PEREGRINE'S HOME FOR PECULIAR CHILDREN by Ransom Riggs

The first thing you find out when yer dog learns to talk is that dogs don't got nothing much to say.

THE KNIFE OF NEVER LETTING GO by Patrick Ness

Our best friend was ash in a jar.

OSTRICH BOYS by Keith Grey

There was a hand in the darkness, and it held a knife.

THE GRAVEYARD BOOK by Neil Gaiman

We went to the moon to have fun, but the moon turned out to completely suck.

FEED by M.T. Anderson

July had been blown out like a candle by a biting wind that ushered in a leaden August sky.
MY FAMILY AND OTHER ANIMALS
by Gerald Durrell

On the morning of its first birthday, a baby was found floating in a cello case in the middle of the English Channel.
ROOFTOPPERS by Katherine Rundell

Johnny never knew for certain why he started seeing the dead.
JOHNNY AND THE DEAD
by Terry Pratchett

Lyra and her daemon moved through the darkening hall, taking care to keep to one side, out of sight of the kitchen.
NORTHERN LIGHTS
by Philip Pullman

When I stepped out into the bright sunlight from the darkness of the movie house, I had only two things on my mind: Paul Newman and a ride home.
THE OUTSIDERS by S.E. Hinton

It was a bright cold day in April, and the clocks were striking thirteen.
1984 by George Orwell

JON WALTER SAYS ...

An opening sentence should draw the reader from their own head and take them somewhere completely different. It's the start of a whole new world and for that reason, probably the most important line of any book.

JON WALTER IS THE AUTHOR OF
CLOSE TO THE WIND AND MY NAME'S NOT FRIDAY.

My father got the dog drunk on cherry brandy at the party last night. If the RSPCA hear about it he could get done.
THE SECRET DIARY OF ADRIAN MOLE, AGED 13¾ by Sue Townsend

NARRATIVE HOOKS

There are different techniques that authors can use to draw readers into a story.

In stories told from a first-person viewpoint, writers can begin the book with the narrator directly addressing the reader. This approach can quickly create a sense of a character's voice and make readers feel involved in the story from the very start.

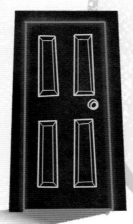

Late in the winter of my seventeenth year, my mother decided I was depressed, presumably because I rarely left the house, spent quite a lot of time in bed, read the same book over and over, ate infrequently, and devoted quite a bit of my abundant free time to thinking about death.
THE FAULT IN OUR STARS
by **John Green**

'Reasons I'd like to stay living at Gran's,' I said as Pia and I left the heat of the August sunshine behind and stepped through the automatic doors into the air-conditioned Village area of Westfield Shopping Mall.
'One I can walk to school from there –'
MILLION DOLLAR MATES
by **Cathy Hopkins**

Another way of giving the reader a sense of different characters' voices is to start a story with dialogue. This can be a great way to set up a situation at the same time as showing how characters respond to this.

In an atmospheric opening, a writer might focus on the description of a specific setting or character. This can help create a specific mood such as an ominous atmosphere and set the tone for the story that follows.

Jack stands in the dark on the landing of the old house, and looks at his feet. He is outside the last of the three doors, the one that is underlined with flickering light. He doesn't move. He stares down at the twin crescents of light reflecting on the toes of his shoes. He looks at the thin highlights along the edges of the bare floorboards and at the pattern of the grain in the wood in the pale puddle of light that leaks under the door.
THIRTEEN CHAIRS by **Dave Shelton**

Starting an opening scene in the middle of the action can create an instant sense of excitement. Without giving too many details about character or setting, a writer can sweep the reader up in the action and make them curious to find out exactly what's going on.

Metal ground against metal; a lurching shudder shook the floor beneath him. He fell down at the sudden movement and shuffled backwards on his hands and feet, drops of sweat beading on his forehead despite the cool air.
THE MAZE RUNNER by James Dashner

Opening a story with a question or unexpected image can intrigue a reader. If you want to try this technique, you will need to craft the perfect opening line.

The piano arrived too late to stop the sky falling in. If it had come earlier, things might have ended on a sweet note. As it was, everything was jangled, unstrung, struck dumb.
THE MIDDLE OF NOWHERE by Geraldine McCaughrean

Whichever technique you choose, make sure the opening scene of your story hooks the reader and keeps them turning the pages.

81

CONFLICT AND COMPLICATIONS

At the heart of every story is conflict. Without this detectives would solve every murder in a mystery before the victims go cold and any star-crossed lovers in a romance would get together without a hitch. Whatever genre of story you are writing, you need to identify the conflicts that drive the plot forward.

GOALS AND OBSTACLES

Authors often start by thinking about what a protagonist wants in a story. This need or desire will inform the actions they take and the way they respond to the situations they face. For instance in *The Lord of the Rings*, Frodo's goal is to reach Mount Doom to destroy the One Ring. Conflict then can arise from an antagonist who has an opposing desire, and in *The Lord of the Rings* this character is Sauron who wants to claim the One Ring for himself.

Remember your protagonist's goal can change as the story progresses.

At the start of *The Hunger Games*, Katniss just wants to keep her family safe, but when she is entered into the games, her new goal is to survive. The obstacles an author places in the path of a protagonist and how they attempt to overcome each of these are the conflicts that stitch a story together.

The longer you can keep your protagonist from achieving their goal will increase the tension.

PLOTTING PROBLEMS

Think about the breakdown of your plot. For each scene, can you identify what your protagonist's goal is at this point in the story? Remember, a character might have an overarching goal that spans the whole of the story, but also need to achieve other goals along the way.

For every scene, work out what problem they face and how they will or won't overcome this.

antagonist *noun*
a person who is hostile to someone or something; an opponent

protagonist *noun*
the chief character in a drama or narrative

TYPES OF CONFLICT

Stories give you the space to explore all kinds of problems and situations, from a teenage boy who doesn't feel like he fits into his own family to invading alien armies waging interplanetary war. Look at these words to help you think about the conflicts you could write about.

WAR

oppression

moral choices

FAMILY PROBLEMS

TECHNOLOGICAL ADVANCES

environmental change

misunderstanding

POLITICAL INSTABILITY

RELATIONSHIPS

racism

coming of age

IDENTITY CRISIS

terrorism

bullying

FEUDS

CHRISTOPHER EDGE SAYS ...

Real life doesn't come with an age rating. Stories help us to make sense of the world, even at its most random and cruel.

CHRISTOPHER EDGE IS THE AUTHOR OF
THE MANY WORLDS OF ALBIE BRIGHT
AND THIS BOOK!

I AGAINST I

Sometimes the conflict can be inside a character's head. Internal conflict is the struggle between what a character wants and the way their thoughts, beliefs or emotions are preventing them from achieving this goal.

Thinking about your protagonist's personality can help you to identify the way you can build internal conflict into your story.

What fears or personality flaws do they have?

How might these conflict with the situations in which you place them?

Forcing your hero or heroine to make hard decisions where they have to battle against their own emotions and beliefs can intensify the drama.

injustice

SACRiFiCE

quests

extremism

REBELLION

personal demons

bereavement

self-discovery

refugees

85

SETTING AND CONFLICT

Sometimes the source of conflict in a story can come from the setting itself. From *Robinson Crusoe* to *The Revenant*, survival stories can depict characters battling against the natural world.

In this type of story drama can come from a character overcoming impossible odds.

Make the struggle matter. Give your character a reason why they're fighting to survive and a final goal that they're trying to reach.

This might be to find their family again or to take revenge on the person who left them for dead.

Dystopian fiction such as *The Hunger Games* presents nightmarish settings where characters live in oppressive societies. Think about why your protagonist doesn't fit into this society to find the conflict that will fuel your story. Although these stories sometimes present future worlds, you can explore contemporary issues such as how technology could take over our lives in the fictional societies you create.

The wounded man stared at the gap in the trees where they had disappeared. His rage was complete, consuming him as fire envelops the needles of a pine. He wanted nothing in the world except to place his hands around their necks and choke the life from them. Instinctively he started to yell out, forgetting again that his throat produced no words, only pain. He raised himself on his left elbow. He could bend his right arm slightly, but it would support no weight. The movement sent agonizing bolts through his neck and back.

THE REVENANT
by Michael Punke

Sixty seconds. That's how long we're required to stand on our metal circles before the sound of a gong releases us. Step off before the minute is up, and land mines blow your legs off. Sixty seconds to take in the ring of tributes all equidistant from the Cornucopia, a giant golden horn shaped like a cone with a curved tail, the mouth of which is at least twenty feet high, spilling over with the things that will give us life here in the arena. Food, containers of water, weapons, medicine, garments, fire starters.

THE HUNGER GAMES
by Suzanne Collins

dystopian *adjective*
to do with an imagined place or situation in which everything is unpleasant or bad

BUILDING TO A CLIMAX

Every story builds to a climax. This is the point in the narrative where the action reaches a peak – from a final confrontation with their deadliest foe to facing up to their innermost fear. Only by conquering the challenge that they face in the story's climax can a protagonist achieve their ultimate goal.

MAKE IT COUNT

The key to creating a satisfying climax is to raise the stakes.

If you're writing a thriller or adventure story, this climatic scene needs to out-action all the scenes that have come before.

In a horror story, the climax needs to place the protagonist in their most frightening situation yet and make the reader feel equally terrified.

Whatever kind of story you are writing, you want to create an intensity of emotion in the story's climax.

" JAMES PATTERSON SAYS ...

I'm big on having a blistering pace. That's one of the hallmarks of what I do, and that's not easy. I never blow up cars and things like that, so it's something else that keeps the suspense flowing. I try not to write a chapter that isn't going to turn on the movie projector in your head.

JAMES PATTERSON IS AN AUTHOR OF ADULT AND YOUNG ADULT FICTION.

"

Rosa May was dragging me towards the edge. Pulling me along, forcing me into the water.

'You'll never be able to leave me now,' she said, wrapping her arms right round me.

'Stop it,' I gasped. 'I can't swim.' The water was icy cold. The air flew out of my lungs. 'Let go of me, Rosa May, please!'

Her voice was soft in my ear. 'I told you I'd find a way to make the summer last for ever.'

I tried to dig my heels in, to push back against her, but it was useless. She was so much stronger than me. I felt limp in her arms. Helpless. She dragged me in deeper, down into the lake, until the water closed over my head.

BUTTERFLY SUMMER by Anne-Marie Conway

CASTING THE CLIMAX

In the climax, the reader's focus needs to be on the protagonist so writers often clear the stage of any superfluous supporting characters. By isolating your hero or heroine and leaving them alone to face their antagonist, you can emphasize the enormity of the challenge they face.

climax *noun*
the most interesting, important or intense point of something

Think Luke Skywalker versus Darth Vader or Harry Potter facing off against Voldemort.

REACH THE PEAK

Think about how you could use some of the ideas below in the climax of your story. You could use more than one to create a climatic scene.

SETBACK
zero hour
catastrophe
CATACLYSM
QUANDARY
reversal DILEMMA
upheaval **adversity**
BACKTRACK

cover-up
divulgence
CROWNING POINT
CULMINATION
CRUNCH **emergency**
finale SMOKING OUT
zenith high spot
turnaround

crux
sticky
CALAMITY
CHANGE OF HEART
U-TURN **shift**
situation rubicon
crossroads
critical point

THE SETTING

You need to signal to the reader that they've reached the climax of the story. Writers sometimes do this by shifting the scene to a new location. Think about how this setting can add to the emotion of this climatic scene. In the final book of *The Lord of the Rings*, the climatic scene unfolds inside Mount Doom as Frodo struggles to achieve the ultimate goal of his quest.

The fires below awoke in anger, the red light blazed, and all the cavern was filled with a great glare and heat. Suddenly Sam saw Gollum's long hands draw upwards to his mouth; his white fangs gleamed, and then snapped as they bit. Frodo gave a cry, and there he was, fallen upon his knees at the chasm's edge. But Gollum, dancing like a mad thing, held aloft the ring, a finger still thrust within its circle. It shone now as if verily it was wrought of living fire.

'Precious, precious, precious!' Gollum cried. 'My Precious! O my Precious!' And with that, even as his eyes were lifted up to gloat on his prize, he stepped too far, toppled, wavered for a moment on the brink, and then with a shriek he fell. Out of the depths came his last wail Precious, and he was gone.
THE RETURN OF THE KING by J. R. R. Tolkien

REVELATION

confession

DISCLOSURE

surprising fact

admission

BROUGHT TO LIGHT

exposure

let slip

leak

moment of truth

ABOUT-FACE

UNMASKED

BETRAYAL

unearthed

DECLARATION

unveiling

REVERSALS AND REVEALS

Just like the plot of the story, a climax should contain twists and turns to build suspense and heighten the tension.

Writers can sometimes use reversals to create a climatic surprise. This is where the protagonist's expectations are suddenly turned on their head. Perhaps a character suddenly reveals that they're not what they seem or a secret is discovered that changes everything ...

Whatever genre of story you're writing, think about how you can turn things upside down. Make sure that any twists you include don't come completely out of left field.

You should seed clues earlier in the story so that this climax feels believable, no matter how big the surprise.

THE MOMENT OF TRUTH

Every moment should have led your lead character to this climatic scene. Every event that has taken place, every experience that has shaped them, has brought them to this point.

In the climax there needs to be a moment of truth for the protagonist where the choice they make reveals their true character. This decision might be the most important one they will ever take – a difficult choice that will change their destiny.

Remember the climax of a story doesn't need to be an epic confrontation. It might be a quiet emotional moment where a character resolves an inner conflict.

Will they succeed in achieving their goal? Or will they fall at the final hurdle? Only you can decide ...

THE PERFECT ENDING

Before a reader puts a book down, an author needs to give them a sense of an ending. The resolution is the final scenes where any loose ends are tied up and the characters can show how they've been changed by the events of the story. It's the calm after the storm of the climax.

NEW BEGINNINGS

In the very best stories characters become real to the reader. After spending so much time in their company, readers can't help but wonder what will happen to them after the final page is turned.

The best endings hint at how the main characters' lives will go on after the end of the story.

In the final chapter of Charlotte Brontë's novel *Jane Eyre*, the heroine marries her true love, Mr Rochester, and at the end of the novel the reader learns that they have been happily married now for ten years.

MICHAEL MORPURGO SAYS ...

Wherever my story takes me, however dark and difficult the theme, there is always some hope and redemption, not because readers like happy endings, but because I am an optimist at heart. I know the sun will rise in the morning, that there is a light at the end of every tunnel.

MICHAEL MORPURGO IS THE AUTHOR OF **WAR HORSE, PRIVATE PEACEFUL** AND MANY MORE BOOKS FOR CHILDREN.

Think about how you can give the reader hints about the future lives of your characters in the final scene of the story.

The bus is already coming down the hill. I grab Mina's hand and start to run. I make a bet – if we get to the stop before the bus, then everything will be OK.

Even now it's hard to walk away, but every time I come home and Mum's still there, it gets easier. At least she's trying. Staying sober: one day at a time.

That's how we live. We have good days and bad days.

But the gaps between the bad ones are getting longer – and that's something.

A good place to start.

We beat the bus by a car's length.
15 DAYS WITHOUT A HEAD by Dave Cousins

ALL THE FEELS

Every writer wants to craft an ending that has emotional impact. This final scene should evoke feelings and emotions that fit in with the story that's been told. Certain genres might generate particular emotions, such as the capture of a killer in a crime story leaving the reader feeling satisfied. Think about the genre of story you are writing and how you want the reader to feel as they read the final page.

HORROR

INCENSED   UPSET   **agitated**   **crushed**
exhilarated   **irate**   seething   fearful   *terrified*   **uneasy**   TENSE
petrified   *troubled*   BRAVE   **anxious**   NERVOUS   SHOCKED
drained   **bewildered**   APPREHENSIVE   *gloomy*   *overwhelmed*
SURPRISED   REVULSION   **scared**   *weird*

SCIENCE FICTION AND FANTASY

ASTOUNDED   AWED   GRATEFUL   *euphoric*   **unburdened**
triumph   **enthralled**   inspired   THRILLED
SURPRISED   **thoughtful**   **content**   **uplifted**
hopeful   **satisfied**   *amazed*   *intrigued*
FASCINATED   **courageous**   OPTIMISTIC   *curious*

CRIME AND THRILLER

SHOCKED   *astonishment*   TEARFUL
enraged   SATISFIED   surprised   **disturbed**
tense   *triumph*   *relief*   nerve-jangled
perplexed   absorbed   BLINDSIDED

COMEDY

delighted HAPPY AMUSED
affection ECSTATIC **empathy**
TICKLED **smiling** laughing
beaming *cheerful* overjoyed
playful *happy-go-lucky* *sunny*

ROMANCE

relief EXHILARATED **optimistic**
SENTIMENTAL SATISFIED hopeful
pleased *blissful* *inspired*
touched LONGING **jealous**
frustration **happy** ELATED
SYMPATHETIC TOLERANT **grateful**
thankful fulfilled content
approving euphoric JUBILANT
passionate

KEEP IT BRIEF

Don't drag the ending out over endless pages. You need to present the reader with a satisfying pay-off that makes the time they've invested in the story feel worthwhile. All loose ends should be tied up quickly. Keeping the resolution tightly focused will maximize the emotional impact of this closing scene.

PATRICK NESS SAYS ...

How you leave the reader is so important — not the climax; I call it the 'exit feeling.'

PATRICK NESS IS THE AUTHOR OF *A MONSTER CALLS.*

What kind of
'exit feeling' do these
endings give you?

SPOILER ALERT!

They were both smiling and they were both crying and it
was true, life would go on. Winter had its damage done
but things would soon heal and be forgotten and gone.
Ennor knew this and it was not wishing or hoping or banking
on luck. It was the truth and as she thought of it she sank
her arm into the water and let go of the picture frame,
two strangers' faces, one and two, and gone for ever.
WINTER DAMAGE by Natasha Carthew

Up ahead of us that pool of sunshine is still there on the
hillside. I don't think I ever seen grass look so green as it
does up there. And we make our way towards it, putting
one foot in front of the other, taking each slow step at
a time, knowing one day that we'll get there.
Some time soon I'll stand in the sunshine.
MY NAME'S NOT FRIDAY by Jon Walter

I stand in this parking lot, realizing that I've never been
this far from home, and here is this girl I love and cannot
follow. I hope this is the hero's errand, because not
following her is the hardest thing I've ever done.
I keep thinking she will get into the car, but she doesn't,
and she finally turns around to me and I see her soaked
eyes. The physical space between us evaporates. We play
the broken strings of our instruments one last time.
I feel her hands on my back. And it is dark as I kiss her,
but I have my eyes open and so does Margo. She is close
enough to me that I can see her, because even now there
is the outward sign of the invisible light, even at night in
this parking lot on the outskirts of Agloe. After we kiss,
our foreheads touch as we stare
at each other. Yes, I can see her
almost perfectly in this cracked
darkness.
PAPER TOWNS by John Green

resolution *noun*
the part of a story where
it comes to an end and
difficulties are resolved

EXIT ONLY

PLOT HOLES AND PROBLEMS

Finishing the first draft of a story is a real achievement. However, when a writer types the final line, they've still got a mountain to climb. To get a book ready for publication an author will revise the story several times until they feel they've got it right.

CRITICAL READER

Some writers reread as they write, beginning each writing session by reviewing what they wrote in the last one. This can help keep the story on track, making sure that the plot progresses in a logical way. Other authors find rereading can slow them down and prefer to get to the end before they look back at what they've written.

STEPHEN KING SAYS ...

When you write a book, you spend day after day scanning and identifying the trees. When you're done, you have to step back and look at the forest.

STEPHEN KING IS A BESTSELLING AUTHOR OF HORROR, FANTASY AND SUPERNATURAL FICTION.

PLOT

PLOT

PLOT

PLOT

Whichever type of writer you are, rereading your first draft is the first chance you have to look at the whole story and check how it's working. It is important that you don't rush into this.

Take a break when you finish your first draft to give your brain space to breathe.

You'll be able to judge what you've written more objectively if you don't jump into rereading straight away.

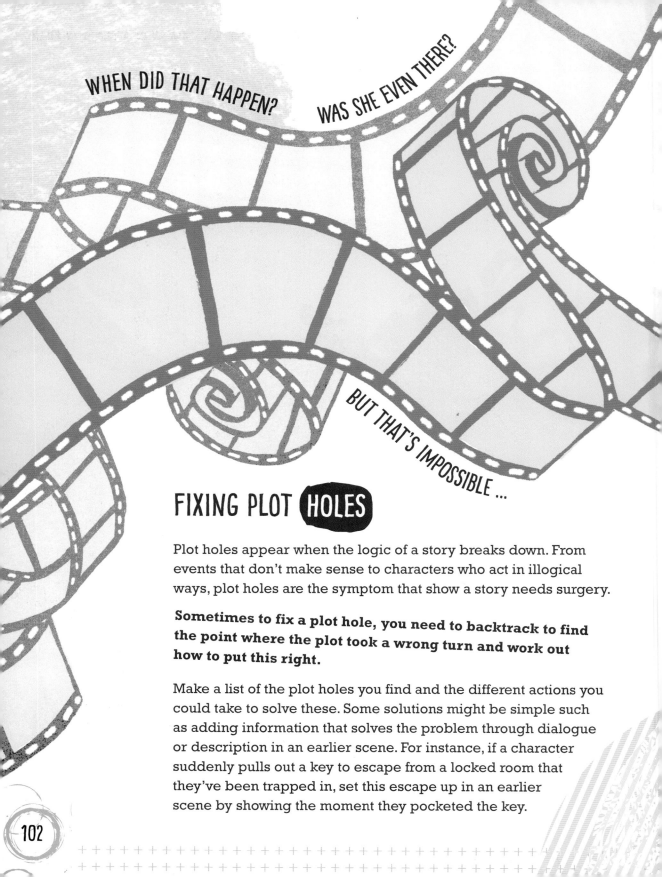

WHEN DID THAT HAPPEN?

WAS SHE EVEN THERE?

BUT THAT'S IMPOSSIBLE ...

FIXING PLOT HOLES

Plot holes appear when the logic of a story breaks down. From events that don't make sense to characters who act in illogical ways, plot holes are the symptom that show a story needs surgery.

Sometimes to fix a plot hole, you need to backtrack to find the point where the plot took a wrong turn and work out how to put this right.

Make a list of the plot holes you find and the different actions you could take to solve these. Some solutions might be simple such as adding information that solves the problem through dialogue or description in an earlier scene. For instance, if a character suddenly pulls out a key to escape from a locked room that they've been trapped in, set this escape up in an earlier scene by showing the moment they pocketed the key.

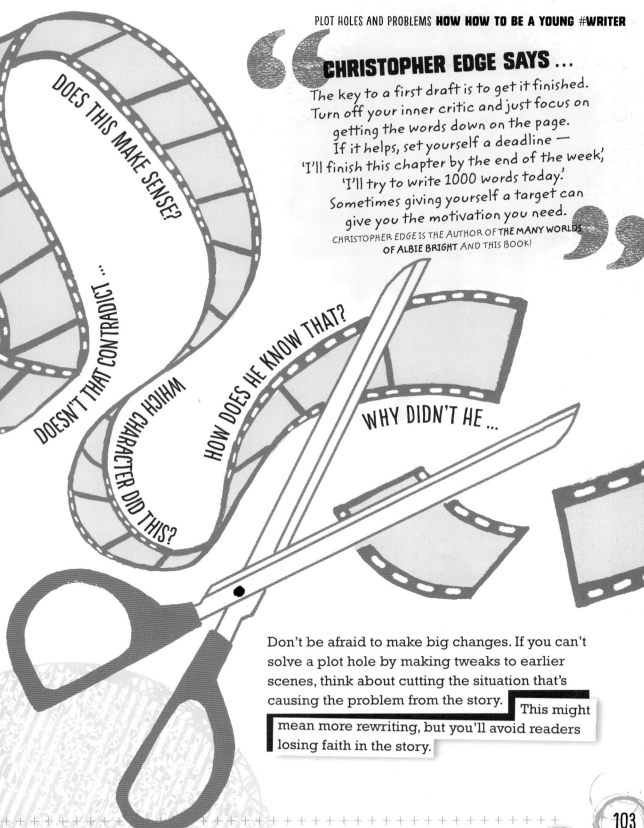

CHRISTOPHER EDGE SAYS ...

The key to a first draft is to get it finished.
Turn off your inner critic and just focus on
getting the words down on the page.
If it helps, set yourself a deadline —
'I'll finish this chapter by the end of the week',
'I'll try to write 1000 words today.'
Sometimes giving yourself a target can
give you the motivation you need.

CHRISTOPHER EDGE IS THE AUTHOR OF *THE MANY WORLDS OF ALBIE BRIGHT* AND THIS BOOK!

DOES THIS MAKE SENSE?

DOESN'T THAT CONTRADICT ...

WHICH CHARACTER DID THIS?

HOW DOES HE KNOW THAT?

WHY DIDN'T HE ...

Don't be afraid to make big changes. If you can't
solve a plot hole by making tweaks to earlier
scenes, think about cutting the situation that's
causing the problem from the story. This might
mean more rewriting, but you'll avoid readers
losing faith in the story.

FIRST DRAFT CHECKLIST

No first draft is ever perfect. Don't sweat the small stuff like spelling mistakes or checking full stops – this stage is all about making sure that the nuts and bolts of your story work.

Print out the story on paper and read it with fresh eyes. Don't make any changes the first time you read it, but make notes of the things that you notice in the margins.

Use this checklist to help you to focus on the important aspects.

✔ Story

Does the story make sense? Are any parts confusing? Can you spot any plot holes?

✔ Structure

Does the story have a clear beginning, middle and end? Does the action develop in a logical way? Is the sequence of events clear to the reader?

✔ Characters

Do the characters seem believable? Is there a strong lead character whose actions and reactions drive the plot forward? Is every character vital to the story or can any be cut?

✔ Conflict

Does the protagonist have a clear goal? Do you show how characters are changed by the challenges they face?

✔ Setting

Do the different settings in the story feel real?
Is there too much description or scene-setting
in any parts of the story? Do any scenes need
more description?

✔ Dialogue

Does what the characters say sound convincing?
Does the dialogue move the plot forward or
reveal something about the characters in the
story? Is it always clear who is talking?

✔ Scenes

Is every scene essential to the story?
Are there any scenes that could be cut?

✔ Pace

Does the pace of the story feel right?
Are there any parts that feel rushed?
Does the action seem to plod at any point?

✔ Ending

Does the story build to a satisfying climax?
Does the ending strike the right emotional note?

◀REVISING AND EDITING

When you've made a plan for what you need to fix, you need to start revising your story. Don't get intimidated by the idea of rewriting the manuscript from scratch. Make this a manageable task by working scene by scene.

UNLEASH YOUR INNER CRITIC

When you're writing a first draft keep your inner critic on a tight rein or you'll never finish the story. But when it comes to rewriting, let them off the leash to sharpen up your prose.

Weigh up every sentence of your story to check that it's expressing what you want it to in the very best way. **Keep a watch out** for any sentences that are too long or that sound clunky when you read them out loud. **Play around** with word order and vocabulary until it sounds right to your ear.

KILL YOUR DARLINGS

You might have written the perfect sentence, but if it doesn't add anything you need to take an axe to it. Editing is all about cutting any parts of the story that don't work – even if you think it's the best thing that you've ever written. Don't despair – you can always create a new file to keep any 'darlings' that don't make the cut. You might have the chance to use them in another story.

EDIT

CUT

REWORK

AXE

CHOP

" ALWYN HAMILTON SAYS ...

Once I have all the words down I sort of treat that like the scaffolding of a draft. I go through and often realize I can cut things or combine two scenes, or that chapter 1 was written with an idea that morphed by the time I got to the end, so fix all that. And then it's a question for me of just going through and getting the actual words themselves right.

ALWYN HAMILTON IS THE AUTHOR OF *REBEL OF THE SANDS*. "

EDITING CHECKLIST

Make sure your story shines
by using this editing checklist
to polish your prose.

☐ Viewpoint and voice

What point of view have you told the story from? Does this change or stay the same? Is the narrative voice consistent?

☐ Repetition

Have you used the same words or phrases too often? Can you use pronouns to avoid repetition of nouns or names? Is any information repeated unnecessarily, even if this is expressed in a different way?

☐ Dialogue

Is dialogue laid out and punctuated correctly? Are dialogue tags and other indicators of which character is speaking used when needed?

☐ Cliché

Can you spot any overused expressions such as 'dead as a doornail'? Can you coin any new metaphors or phrases to express these ideas in different ways?

☐ Spelling and punctuation

Proofread to make sure the spelling and punctuation is accurate. A spellchecker won't pick up every mistake, so read carefully to make sure you've used the right word in the right place.

☐ Adverbs and adjectives

Look at every adverb. Can you use a different verb to express the action more precisely? Do you need all the adjectives that you've used? Have you chosen the best ones to create vivid images in a reader's mind?

" NICK HORNBY SAYS ...

Go on, young writers — treat yourself to a joke, or an adverb! Spoil yourself! Readers won't mind!

NICK HORNBY IS AN AUTHOR OF ADULT AND YOUNG ADULT FICTION.

" JOE CRAIG SAYS ...

Make every line count — for the story, not for its own beauty. Challenge every word. Every. Single. Word.

JOE CRAIG IS THE AUTHOR OF THE **JIMMY COATES** SERIES.

CRITICAL READER

Before a book hits the shelves, an editor will read every word and give an author feedback to help them get the story right.

Get a second opinion on your story from someone that you trust.

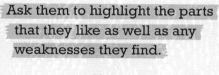

Ask them to highlight the parts that they like as well as any weaknesses they find.

If they have any comments for improvements that you could make, listen carefully to these.

CHOOSING A TITLE

Some authors, like the bestselling crime writer Ian Rankin, can't begin to write a new novel until they've decided on the title. Other authors leave choosing a title until they get to the end of the story or even let their publisher suggest this. But if you want your story to stand out from the crowd, you need to choose a title with real shelf appeal.

THE LONG AND THE SHORT OF IT

From attention-grabbing titles that scream 'Look at me!' to intriguing titles that stick in the memory, there are many different ways to create a great title.

Single-word titles such as *Neverwhere*, *Holes* and *Uglies* can be eye-catching and easy to remember, but you need to make sure that you choose a distinctive word that reflects what the book is about.

Sometimes longer titles such as *Miss Peregrine's Home for Peculiar Children* can make a book sound unique, but think about the length of the title and how this sounds when you read it aloud. If it's more than a mouthful, the chances are you won't be able to fit the title on the cover of the book.

TITLE INSPIRATION

The inspiration for many titles can be found inside the pages of the story.

Sometimes the lead character's name can be used as the title such as *Coraline* by Neil Gaiman or maybe just as part of the title as in the Harry Potter books by J. K. Rowling. Titles based on places such as *Wuthering Heights* and *Treasure Island* can give the reader an immediate picture of the story's setting, but make sure this location is central to the story.

Some authors like to choose a title that reflects the themes of the book. Think about classic novels like *Pride and Prejudice* or *War and Peace*. However if you choose big themes for your title you need to make sure that the story you tell lives up to these! Key moments and lines from the story can also find their way into the title – *To Kill A Mockingbird* is taken from a line of dialogue, whilst *The Hunger Games* is named after the event at the heart of the story.

MALORIE BLACKMAN SAYS ...

'Double Cross' seemed an appropriate title as it describes what Tobey sets out to do, which is double cross both the Nought organized crime leader Alex McAuley and the Cross organized crime family, the Dowds. But in the end, Tobey ends up double-crossing himself.

MALORIE BLACKMAN IS THE AUTHOR OF NOUGHTS AND CROSSES SERIES INCLUDING DOUBLE CROSS.

QUOTES AND LYRICS

Some authors look for inspiration for titles from songs, plays, poems or even other books. Brian Conaghan's Young Adult novel *The Bombs that Brought Us Together* was inspired by a lyric in the song 'Ask' by The Smiths. Perhaps there's a song that soundtracks a moment in your story or a lyric that captures an important theme?

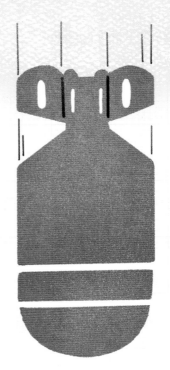

The title of Ray Bradbury's novel *Something Wicked This Way Comes* is taken from Shakespeare's play *Macbeth*, whilst *Of Mice and Men* by John Steinbeck comes from a line of poetry by Robert Burns.

Don't just choose a quotation because you think it sounds cool – any line or phrase that you pick should capture something important about the story.

GENRE EXPECTATIONS

From **horror** to **mystery**, **spy thrillers** to **supernatural fantasy**, you'll often find certain words or phrases cropping up in specific genres of books. Think about what kind of story you'd expect to read from the title *The Queen's Poisoner* or which genre might be suggested by a title which contains the words 'Demons', 'Death' and 'Blood'. Take a look at online bestseller lists to see which words appear in the genre you are writing in.

If your title doesn't meet your reader's expectations, you're giving them an excuse not to pick up your book.

Remember though that the best titles don't follow trends, but set them! Sometimes giving typical images a twist can help to create an original title, such as the title of Carrie Ryan's post-apocalyptic zombie novel, *The Forest of Hands and Teeth*. And if you're writing a trilogy, you might want to choose titles that create a brand for your series in a similar way to Veronica Roth's science fiction adventure trilogy, *Divergent*, *Insurgent* and *Allegiant*.

RESEARCH

When you've got a list of possible titles for your story, type these into a search engine. You might find that someone else has already used this title, but unless this has been a bestseller you shouldn't worry too much about this. You can't copyright a title, so if you still think this is the best title for your book – go for it!

Every author wants to be read by as many readers as possible. Try not to choose an embarrassing title that will turn readers off or stop a bookshop or library from putting it on the shelf.

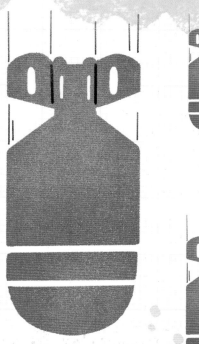

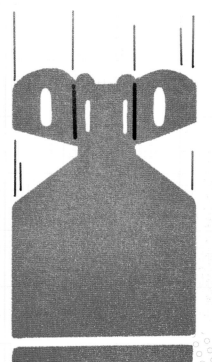

NATASHA DESBOROUGH SAYS...

I settled on the book title 'Weirdos and Camel Toes' because it was cheeky, funny, relevant, flowed beautifully and I knew it would stand out on a book shelf. But whilst I congratulated myself on my eye-catching front cover, I soon discovered that a lot of important people in the industry thought the title was too 'rude and risqué'.

NATASHA DESBOROUGH IS THE AUTHOR OF **WEIRDOS VS QUIMBOIDS** AND **WEIRDOS VS BUMSKULLS**.

BEATING WRITER'S BLOCK

Nearly every author faces a time when they find themselves staring at a blank page without a clue what to write. Suffering from writer's block might mean you've run out of ideas or maybe just taken a wrong turn in your story and don't know how to get it going again.

SPACE TO THINK

Many writers find that giving themselves space to think can unblock their writing. From taking the dog for a walk to a workout session at the gym, moving away from the page or the computer screen can help your brain beat writer's block.

CHRIS D'LACEY SAYS ...

Stuck? Don't burn, shred or feed your manuscript to the hamster. Take a break from the story and listen to your subconscious. Follow up any peculiar ideas it's urging you to explore. If all else fails, try talking the story through with a friend.

CHRIS D'LACEY IS THE AUTHOR OF THE LAST DRAGON CHRONICLES.

WRITING PARTNERS AND GROUPS

Sometimes having someone to discuss your writing with can help you to get unstuck. Find a friend who also likes writing or think about joining a writing group. Sharing your story with others and reading out your work in progress can give you helpful feedback and generate new ideas.

SILENCE YOUR INNER CRITIC

When you're writing, there might be moments where your inner critic gets the upper hand. Try not to listen to any negative thoughts about your writing and focus on the story you want to tell. There'll be time at the end to polish your writing, but the important thing now is to get the words on the page. Write down your worries and file them for later when you start on the edit.

AVOIDING WRITER'S BLOCK

The best strategy for avoiding writer's block is to stop writing when you know what's coming next. At the end of every writing session make a few notes outlining the next event in the story. That way, you'll be able to pick up where you left off.

If you feel that your story is running out of steam, try changing the way you work. Switch from screen to paper or vice versa to spark your writing into life.

Sometimes rewriting the scene where your writing got stuck can unlock the problem and let you power on with the plot.

If not, you can always park this scene to one side and write a different scene where you know exactly what happens.

ANGIE SAGE SAYS ...

Send in a totally new and unexpected character. If this character arrives in a dramatic way, you will have something fun to write about and you will probably find that once again ideas begin to appear.

ANGIE SAGE IS THE AUTHOR OF THE **SEPTIMUS HEAP** AND **ARAMINTA SPOOK** SERIES.

Even fictional characters can suffer from writer's block ...

Penelope stared down at the blank sheet of paper in front of her, its expanse of perfect whiteness an unconquered continent of story. She felt like Captain Scott staring out from the prow of the Discovery at the looming Antarctic coastline, strange mountains of ice barring the way to his goal. Penny sighed, her gaze slipping sideways to the wastepaper basket beside her desk. Balls of crumpled paper spilled out from this, the unfinished sentences scrawled across each one a journal of her failure to capture even a foothold in this new tale she was trying to craft from the pen of Montgomery Flinch.

THE BLACK CROW CONSPIRACY by Christopher Edge

GETTING YOUR STORY OUT THERE

Every author writes to be read. Whether you want to see your book at the top of the bestseller charts or just want to share your story with like-minded readers, there are lots of different paths you can follow to try to get your writing published.

FIND A PUBLISHER

Take a walk around a bookshop and find the section that best fits the genre of your story. This might be crime, horror, fantasy, science fiction, romance, Young Adult or maybe even something else. Note down the publishers who publish in this section. You'll find the publisher's address and very often their website given inside the book on the imprint page.

Take a look at the publishers' websites to find out if they are looking for submissions from new authors. Many publishers will only take a look at a manuscript if it comes to them via a literary agent, but a few still look through their slush pile of unsolicited manuscripts to try and find great new stories. Follow their submission guidelines to give your manuscript the best chance of making it out of the slush pile.

GET AN AGENT

Just like a football agent who gets their star player a contract with a Champions League club, a literary agent represents authors and tries to find the best publisher for their books. One advantage of getting a literary agent is that they know which publishers are on the lookout for the type of story you have written. An agent can get your manuscript read by the right person and, if the publisher then wants to publish your book, your agent will negotiate the best agreement and take a cut of any money you earn from this.

You can find lists of literary agents in books like the *Writers' & Artists Yearbook* which you can find in most libraries. Just like looking for a potential publisher, research which types of authors a particular agent represents to decide whether they might be interested in your story.

THE APPROACH

Whether you're approaching an agent or a publisher, you need to present yourself and your story in a professional way. Most agents and publishers who are accepting new submissions will ask for a **covering letter** or **email**, a **synopsis of the story** and a **few sample chapters**. This will give them enough information to decide whether they want to read the rest of the story.

THE COVERING LETTER

This is your chance to introduce yourself and the manuscript you are sending. Keep this brief but make sure you include the title of your book, what genre it belongs to and roughly how many words long it is.

In a sentence or two, try to sum up the story. Think about this as your elevator pitch, so try to summarize your story in a snappy and appealing way that will intrigue an agent or publisher and make them keen to read more.

Explain whether the book you have written is a one-off novel or the start of a series you have planned. Finally, give a little bit of information about yourself – especially any details that show your skills as an author – so if you're a book blogger with your own YouTube channel make sure you mention this.

THE SYNOPSIS

A synopsis is a summary of your book. This isn't a chapter-by-chapter breakdown of the plot where you list every single thing that happens in the story.

Think about the synopsis as an extended blurb, but one that explains what happens at the end too.

Try to keep the synopsis to a single page, introducing characters, setting and the key events of the plot. Write it in the present tense, even if your story is written in the past tense. You want the agent or publisher to pick up your manuscript, so write your synopsis in a way that makes this impossible to resist.

SAMPLE CHAPTERS

Agents and publishers get bombarded with manuscripts, so make sure you stay in their good books by sending exactly what they ask for. If an agent asks to see the first three chapters, don't send them chapter four as well just because this includes your favourite part of the story!

Make sure you present the sample chapters you send in the right way.

Start with a title page that includes the book title, your author name and contact details. Each chapter should start on a new page and the text should be double-spaced and justified only on the left-hand side. Number the pages and include your name and the title of the book on each of these too.

GET READY FOR REJECTION

Even the most famous and accomplished authors have experienced rejection. *Harry Potter and the Philosopher's Stone* by J. K. Rowling was rejected by twelve different publishers before an editor at Bloomsbury decided to take a chance on this magical tale.

If your sample chapters come flying back with a rejection note, don't get disheartened. Keep a record of any feedback you get. Agents, editors and publishers are busy people, so if someone has taken time to drop you a line of advice, try to learn from this. A successful author is one who tries to improve all the time. Use rejection as inspiration to turn yourself into a better writer.

Rejection!

Sorry ...

Thanks but no thanks ...

BRYONY PEARCE SAYS ...

Every time I got a rejection, I allowed myself a day to feel really, really despondent. Then I picked myself up and said, 'Right, you've got to do a rewrite.' And that's basically what I did ... I think you have to be so stubborn, so thick-skinned and persistent and willing to rewrite.

BRYONY PEARCE IS THE AUTHOR OF THE YOUNG ADULT NOVEL **ANGEL'S FURY** AND THE **PHOENIX RISING** SERIES.

SHARING STORIES

Another way to reach readers is to take your fiction online. Story sharing apps and websites like Wattpad allow authors to post their stories for free. Millions of readers can read them chapter by chapter and leave comments and feedback. This can be a great way of building a fan base for your fiction. When teenage author Beth Reekles' story *The Kissing Booth* hit 19 millions reads on Wattpad she got a three-book deal from a major publisher.

SELF PUBLISHING

Some authors like to DIY and choose to self-publish their books. Using self-publishing platforms, authors can take charge of every step of the process of publishing an ebook from cover design to choosing the price that it's sold at. Rachel Abbot has sold over a million copies of her self-published novels, whilst Cornelia Funke has also tried her hand at self-publishing.

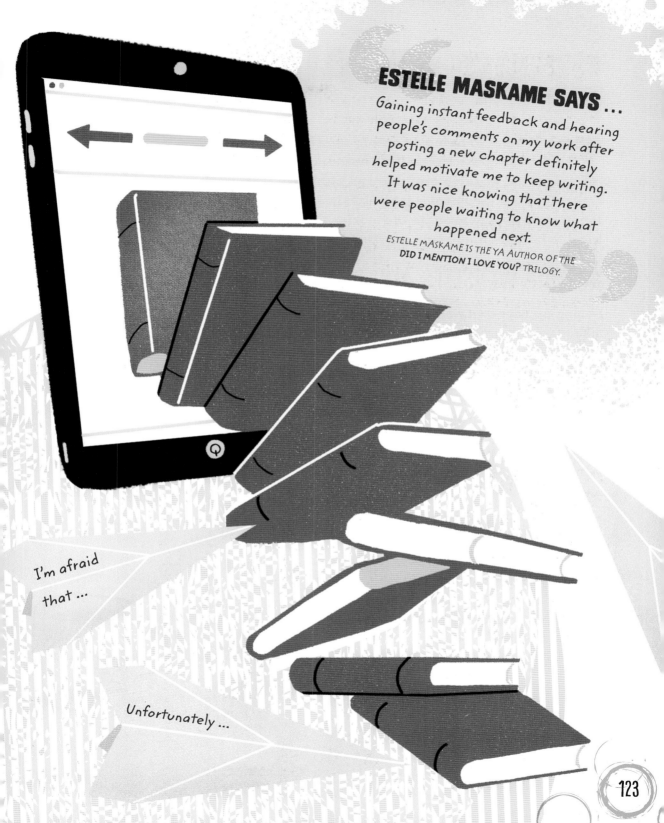

ESTELLE MASKAME SAYS ...

Gaining instant feedback and hearing people's comments on my work after posting a new chapter definitely helped motivate me to keep writing. It was nice knowing that there were people waiting to know what happened next.

ESTELLE MASKAME IS THE YA AUTHOR OF THE **DID I MENTION I LOVE YOU?** TRILOGY.

I'm afraid that ...

Unfortunately ...

BEING AN AUTHOR

There's more to being an author than just writing a book. Nowadays bestselling authors are expected to travel the world to promote and publicize their work. Over a million new books are published every year, so if you want people to share the stories that you write you need to help them to stand out from the crowd.

AUTHOR WEBSITES AND BLOGS

Setting up your own website or blog can act as a shop window for your writing. Here you can share information about yourself and the stories that you write.

You could include sample chapters from your latest stories to try to hook potential new readers.

Look at the websites of any authors you admire and think about any features they include that you could use on your own website.

Many writers use blogs to share their experiences, talking about how they write and their life as a writer. Others use their blogs to share their thoughts about the issues that matter to them. Whatever you choose to write about, make sure the writing on your blog matches the quality of your fiction.

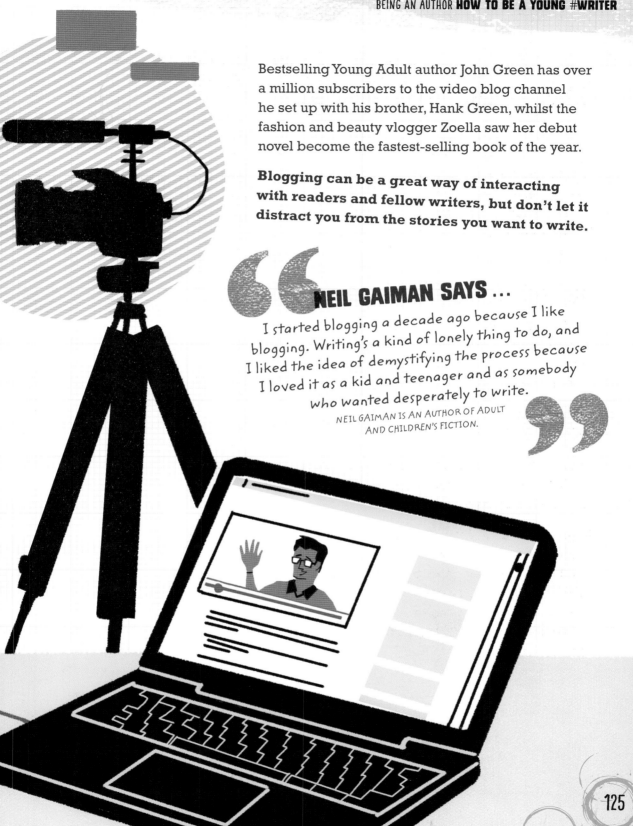

Bestselling Young Adult author John Green has over a million subscribers to the video blog channel he set up with his brother, Hank Green, whilst the fashion and beauty vlogger Zoella saw her debut novel become the fastest-selling book of the year.

Blogging can be a great way of interacting with readers and fellow writers, but don't let it distract you from the stories you want to write.

" NEIL GAIMAN SAYS ...

I started blogging a decade ago because I like blogging. Writing's a kind of lonely thing to do, and I liked the idea of demystifying the process because I loved it as a kid and teenager and as somebody who wanted desperately to write.

NEIL GAIMAN IS AN AUTHOR OF ADULT AND CHILDREN'S FICTION.

newspaper stories

sample chapters

magazine articles

COMPETITIONS

BLOGS

book trailer

BLOG TOUR

RADIO

reviews

giveaways

signing

vlogging

Q&A

chats

THINK OF THE DIFFERENT WAYS YOU CAN PROMOTE YOUR STORIES

PLAYLISTS

business cards

author hangouts

interviews

author website

INTERNET

press release

reading

author biography

SNEAK PREVIEWS

ONLINE COMMUNITIES

merchandise

GET NETWORKING

Social networks such as *Facebook* and *Twitter* are another route to find readers. Successful writers have a ready-made audience, but if you want to find your own followers and fans you need to share interesting content.

From updates about the state of your latest story to links to fascinating articles and videos, think about how you can make connections with fellow readers and writers. On Twitter use hashtags like #writingtips and #fridayreads to find and share writing advice and recommend your favourite reads. Remember these are *social* networks, so don't treat your Facebook page and Twitter feed like a one-way street – engage and interact with others to feel part of a larger community.

Some authors find using social networks can inspire their fiction. David Mitchell's novel *Slade House* grew out of a short story, 'The Right Sort', that he shared on Twitter one tweet at a time. Other writers set up Pinterest accounts where they gather together inspirational images and links.

hashtags

twitter

book tour

CONTESTS

newsletter

EXTRA CONTENT

ESTELLE MASKAME SAYS ...

Using social media to promote my work means that I've got a close connection with my readers, especially now, because they've been with me since the early days. Twitter also has an amazing community of other aspiring writers and book bloggers. It's incredible the way people across social media can interact simply because of our love for writing and reading.

ESTELLE MASKAME IS THE AUTHOR OF THE *DID I MENTION I LOVE YOU?* TRILOGY.

BOOK REVIEWS AND INTERVIEWS ★★★☆☆

Every author dreams of opening up a newspaper to find a rave review of their latest book or sitting in a TV studio to talk about their life as a writer. However, if you want to spread the word about your stories you need a publicity plan.

Think about the different ways you could promote yourself and your writing. From newspapers and magazines to book blogs and podcasts, there are lots of different publications and places that feature new books and writers.

Is there an interesting angle to your book that might interest a journalist?

Maybe the plot is based on a local legend or deals with an issue that is in the news? Make a list of the people you could contact and the ways you could interest them in the book.

Book bloggers are passionate champions of the stories that they love. Take a look at any bloggers who review the kind of book that you've written. Check out whether they accept review copies directly from authors and, if they do, get in touch. Be polite and keep your email brief, asking if they'd like a copy of your book. Book bloggers get bombarded with books, so don't be disappointed if they say no.

Podcasts and video logs can give you the chance to talk about your writing. Why not get a friend to interview you about your latest story or give a reading of the opening chapter? This will be excellent practice for when you write a bestseller and you get invited on the breakfast show sofa!

CHRIS RIDDELL SAYS ...

I love literary festivals because they are places where authors get to meet other authors and share their experiences.

CHRIS RIDDELL IS A CHILDREN'S WRITER AND ILLUSTRATOR.

TALKS AND READINGS

From literary festivals to talks in bookshops and libraries, there's an audience out there who love to hear writers speak.

If you get the chance to see one of your favourite authors in person, go along to see how they do it.

Some authors give talks tailored around their latest book while others provide creative writing workshops to inspire new writers.

Think about where your talents lie and practise your skills. You could offer to give a talk about your latest book at the local library or bookshop. If you decide to read a section from the story as part of your talk, make sure you choose an exciting bit and practise reading this out loud.

WRITING A SERIES

Sometimes the story an author wants to tell is bigger than a single book. *The Lord of the Rings trilogy* by J. R. R. Tolkien contains nearly half a million words, whilst J. K. Rowling's Harry Potter series runs to seven books. If you want to spend more time in the fictional world you have created, writing a series can give you the space to tell all the stories you want to.

WHAT TYPE OF SERIES

Some series like *The Hunger Games* have an overarching plot where the story comes to a natural end in the final book, whilst other series can continue forever as the same lead character sets off on a new adventure in every book.

Decide what kind of series you want to write.

Think about whether the starting point for your series is a story idea which has a definite end or a character or setting which could inspire lots of different plots.

CHARACTERS AND SETTINGS

From fictional detectives who get their name above the title of each book to fantasy heroes and heroines who embark on epic quests, readers want intriguing characters whom they can follow through a series. Think about the characters who will take the leading role in your series. Will their personality stay roughly the same like Batman's does in every comic book or will they be dramatically changed by the events of the story?

The fictional world needs to be rich enough to sustain more than a single story. The *His Dark Materials* trilogy by Philip Pullman takes readers through a series of parallel universes, whilst crime series are sometimes set in a single location with a detective investigating the different crimes that take place there. Make sure you think about the scope of your fictional world and the key settings that will appear in each book in your series.

PLANS AND TIMELINES

Before they begin to write the first book, an author needs to have an idea of the shape of the series. This doesn't mean they know every detail of the plot, but they can think how the story breaks down into different books. Thinking about the sequence of events can help identify where each book begins and ends.

If you're planning a trilogy, you need to think about the ultimate end of the overall story as well as how each individual book will reach a climax. Do you want to end the first book on a cliffhanger like Patrick Ness does at the end of *The Knife of Never Letting Go?* Authors often try to balance giving the reader a sense of satisfaction with making them eager to read the next book in the series. Keep a record of the key events that take place and the characters involved in them. This can help you to avoid any continuity errors by having a character in Book Three start talking about an event in Book One that they couldn't know about.

Making notes about characters and settings can help you to make sure that you describe these in a consistent way in every book.

JANE LAWES SAYS ...

It's much better to put all of your effort into writing one really good book, and just sketching out a few ideas for further stories, than writing the whole series. Chances are your ideas will change a lot, anyway, so your time is better spent making the first book as good as it can be.

JANE LAWES IS A CHILDREN'S WRITER AND AUTHOR OF THE **BALLET STARS** AND **GYM STARS** SERIES.

CHRISTOPHER EDGE SAYS ...

When I was writing *The Many Worlds of Albie Bright*, I had to keep five different parallel worlds inside my head and different parallel versions of the same character! Thinking about the back story — the events that have shaped your characters — can help you to understand their motivations.

CHRISTOPHER EDGE IS THE AUTHOR OF **THE MANY WORLDS OF ALBIE BRIGHT** AND THIS BOOK!

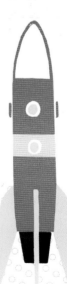

WRITING A PLAY

From comedy to tragedy, there's no limit to the kinds of stories that can be told on a stage. Writing a play is all about using language to bring the drama of a story to life in a way that will engage and entertain a theatre audience.

KNOW THE FORM

You might know how to tell a great story on the page, but to write a play script you need to know how this could be translated to the stage. Reading play scripts and regularly visiting the theatre can help you to understand how different plays work. Comparing novels that have been adapted for the stage such as *The Curious Incident of the Dog in the Night-Time* can help you to understand the differences between these two forms.

COMEDY

farce

theatre

dance

KITCHEN

MODERNIST

MELODRAMA

TRAGEDY

street theatre   epic

MORALITY PLAY

REALISM

POST-MODERN

DRAMA

performance   tragicomedy   REVENGE TRAGEDY

avant-garde

CHARACTERS AND DIALOGUE

The key ingredient of every play is the dialogue. This can reveal characters' personalities and communicate their emotions and ideas, as well as delivering information that helps drive the plot of the play forward.

Playwrights also use dialogue to create atmosphere, with the words character say and the way they speak these setting the tone of a scene.

Many writers speak their scripts out loud as they write, thinking about the rhythm of the dialogue and how natural this sounds. Stage directions describing

a character's actions can be used for emphasis, but some actors prefer to decide how they will deliver a line. Don't forget the importance of silence too.

Sometimes a character's silence can communicate as much as a whole page of dialogue.

Unlike writing a novel where you have an unlimited budget, think about how the play might be staged. Try to limit the number of characters you include. The more actors that are needed, the more money it costs to put on a professional production of the play.

parody
multimedia
MYTH
MIME
musical theatre
OPERA
FRINGE
sink
one-act play
youth theatre
POLITICAL THEATRE
naturalistic drama

LUCINDA COXON SAYS ...

Dialogue is the words characters speak to themselves, one another and an audience. And before that, of course, to the writer. When characters speak to the writer with tremendous urgency, that urgency translates into dialogue with real tension and immediacy.

LUCINDA COXON IS A PLAYWRIGHT AND SCREENWRITER WHOSE PLAYS HAVE BEEN STAGED AROUND THE WORLD.

STAGING AND SETTINGS

The audience's imagination will take them anywhere even with a bare theatre stage – from a spaceship's interior to the heart of an enchanted wood, a medieval king's court to a 21st century block of flats.

Playwrights use stage directions to give instructions to actors, directors and backstage crew about when and where each scene in a play takes place and what this setting looks like.

It's important that these instructions are clear and concise, so that these key people can easily understand them. When writing a play, think about the stage directions you include and how these can help to create the illusion that the world on stage is real. For example, a single chair could be used to indicate a police interrogation room.

PROMPT

STAGE LEFT

STAGE RIGHT

upstage

downstage

line

offstage

exit

" DAVID WOOD SAYS ...

Restrictions on cast size and staging possibilities are not necessarily a bad thing. Well-defined parameters within which to work can be a help, not a hindrance. "

DAVID WOOD OBE IS A DRAMATIST AND PLAYWRIGHT.

rehearsal

entrance

read through

CUE

PLAY TO PRODUCTION

Once you've got it on the page, you need to find a way to get your play onto the stage. Look out for competitions to find new playwrights. These are sometimes advertised online, but make sure the competition is legitimate before you enter it.

Local theatre and drama groups are often on the lookout for new material so see if they would be interested in staging your play. This can give you the chance to work with actors and directors and help you to become a better playwright.

WRITING A 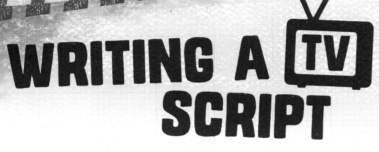 TV SCRIPT

Stories are the lifeblood of television. From one-off dramas to box-set series, sitcoms to soap operas, TV scriptwriters tell different stories in every possible genre. Think about the TV dramas that have you hitting series record and the way these keep you watching.

HOOKING THE VIEWER

You can't switch channels when you watch a film at the cinema, but every TV comes with a remote control. Whatever type of TV programme they are writing, a television scriptwriter has to create an opening sequence that will hook the viewer right from the start. In the BBC drama *Doctor Who* this sequence is usually shown before the opening credits and typically introduces the threat that the Doctor will be facing in this episode.

Think about how you can create a dynamic opening for the TV drama you are writing.

> **What is the most dramatic scene you could show to keep the viewer at home glued to their seat?**

Remember this doesn't need to be from the beginning of the storyline. Some scriptwriters create opening sequences that show a dramatic moment from near the climax and then flash-back with the rest of the drama showing how the plot reached this point.

SCENE BREAKDOWN

Many TV scriptwriters create a scene breakdown to plan out the plot of every episode. In a continuing drama such as a TV soap or detective series, different plot lines might develop over several episodes, whilst in a one-off drama the entire plot might be wrapped up within sixty minutes.

Scriptwriters think carefully about the way scenes are sequenced. To stop the drama seeming predictable, the setting might switch between indoor and outdoor locations with action scenes followed by quieter and more reflective moments.

Just like in any form of storytelling, scriptwriters need to think about the mood created in different scenes.

The best TV drama will vary the scenes to create a fast-paced watch.

SALLY WAINWRIGHT SAYS ...

I will spend a week or two doing a scene breakdown and then the dialogue is the fun bit which takes about a week.

SALLY WAINWRIGHT IS A DIRECTOR, PRODUCER AND BAFTA-WINNING SCREENWRITER OF TV DRAMAS INCLUDING *SCOTT & BAILEY, LAST TANGO IN HALIFAX* AND *HAPPY VALLEY.*

CHARACTER CONNECTIONS

From Sherlock to Homer Simpson, memorable characters make unmissable TV. Think about how you can create characters in your drama that viewers will want to spend time with. **Remember, the audience doesn't have to like every character they see,** but the way a writer portrays them on the page can make viewers eager to find out what will happen to them on screen. Certain genres typically include specific types of characters, such as a detective as the lead character in a crime drama. Try to create distinctive characters that don't feel like copies of ones that have gone before.

ACTION AND DIALOGUE

Some people say that actions speak louder than words, but in TV drama action and dialogue work together to deliver great stories. When writing a TV screenplay, screenwriters use directions to indicate the action, such as GENE LEAPS INTO THE DRIVER'S SEAT AND THE CAR SCREECHES AWAY, with different characters' dialogue introduced by their name in capital letters. You can look at TV screenplays on websites such as the BBC Writer's Room to see how these are set out.

1 EXT. HOSPITAL.

The sound of an ambulance siren in the distance.

2 INT. ACCIDENT & EMERGENCY WARD

An angry-looking young man bangs his fist on the desk of the nurses' station.

STEVE
Nearly an hour I've been waiting!
I could be bleeding to death here!

He shakes his other hand in the faces of the nurses manning the station, showing the blood-soaked bandage round his wrist.

NURSE
And if you take a seat, you'll be seen as soon as possible.

Doors slam open as medics wheel an accident victim on a trolley into A&E.

MEDIC
I need a crash team down here NOW!

GETTING SEEN ON SCREEN

Sometimes DVDs and Blu-rays of TV series include 'making of' documentaries. Take a look to see what these say about the process of writing for TV. Practise writing your own episodes of the TV dramas that you love.

Look for opportunities to break into the world of TV such as screenplay writing competitions advertised on websites such as the BBC Writer's Room.

WRITING A FILM SCREENPLAY

A film screenplay is not a finished story, but the first step on the road to making a movie. Whether this is a Hollywood blockbuster or a film that you could make in the back garden with your friends, the screenplay is the plan that the director will follow to turn the words on the page into moving pictures.

WHAT MAKES A MOVIE?

All stories have a beginning, a middle and an end, but when it comes to making films directors like to talk about 'acts' instead. The structure of most movies can be broken down into three acts: set-up, confrontation and resolution.

❶ Set-up

This first act establishes the main characters and sets up the dramatic situation that will fuel the plot of the film. In *Batman Begins* the opening scenes show how Bruce Wayne's parents were brutally murdered in front of him when he was only a young boy, and this is the event that inspires him to fight crime and eventually become Batman.

❷ Confrontation

This second act is the main part and lasts for the longest time. Just like in a novel or short story, the scenes will depict the conflict and obstacles the protagonist faces that stops them from immediately achieving their goal. In the film *Toy Story* this is the dramatic journey that Woody and Buzz make and the dangers they face to try to get back to Andy.

❸ Resolution

This is the climax to the film. This might be a final showdown between the protagonist and their arch-enemy or the final scenes where the hero or heroine achieves their goal at last.

Take a look at your favourite films and see if you can break the action down into these three acts. Can you spot the scene where each new act begins? Think about how you could structure the script of your story in a similar way.

In the film *E.T. the Extra-Terrestrial*, Elliott's discovery of E.T. is the dramatic situation that launches the next stage of the plot.

INT. ELLIOTT'S ROOM – DAY

Elliott moves into the room from out of the closet. E.T. follows him. He has a blanket wrapped around him.

ELLIOTT
Come on. Don't be afraid. It's all right. Come on. Come on. Come on. Come on. Come on.

They stand looking at each other.

ELLIOTT
Do you talk? You know, talk?

E.T. is silent.

ELLIOTT
Me human. Boy. Elliott. Ell-ee-utt Elliott.

SOUND AND VISION

Movies are made for a big screen, so screenwriters need to tell a story visually. In a scene where the hero is trying to defuse a bomb, a glance at a ticking clock can show that this is a race against time. If you're writing a romcom, think about the visual clues you could give the audience that two characters are in love without using any dialogue.

Screenwriters can use different techniques to give information or build atmosphere. Take a look at the opening of the Pixar film *Up* where a montage of different images tells the story of Carl's life wordlessly. As you break down the plot of your film into scenes, picture what you want the audience to see. You should also include sound effects to tell the story.

SHANE MEADOWS SAYS ...

You never write the perfect script straight away. Don't ever send a first draft of anything to anybody. I would totally advise against it. Because you believe it's fantastic, the minute that somebody reads it they can generally pull it apart. So I think the secret is, prepare yourself for a long haul when you are writing. It takes a long time to whittle your characters down and whittle your story down to something that is important.

SHANE MEADOWS IS A SCREENWRITER
WHOSE FILMS INCLUDE THIS IS ENGLAND.

GET THE RIGHT FORMAT

Professional screenwriters use special scriptwriting software to help them set out their screenplays in the right way. However, if you take a look at some real-life film scripts you can copy their format using an ordinary word-processing package.

DID YOU KNOW?

Most screenplays use a size 12 Courier New font with one A4 page of script equalling one-minute of screen time.

The typical film is approximately two hours long so this means you should aim for 120 pages of script.

Every scene starts with a heading that tells the reader where and when the scene takes place. The abbreviations 'INT' for 'Interior' and 'EXT' for 'Exterior' indicate whether a scene is set inside or outside, along with the exact location and time of the action. Some screenwriters include specific camera shots such as 'CLOSE-UP', but others let the director make these decisions.

WRITING FOR RADIO

If a writer wants to hear their words brought to life by fantastic actors and create drama then they might try writing for radio.

IGNITING IMAGINATIONS

The drama takes place inside the listener's imagination so there is no limit to where a story can be set. *The Hitchhiker's Guide to the Galaxy* began life as a radio drama and went on to be turned into books, videogames, a TV series and film.

Some radio dramas are one-off programmes which can last between fifteen minutes and an hour, whilst other stories are told in multi-part series.

Take a listen to different radio dramas and think about which format would fit the story you want to tell.

AL SMITH SAYS ...

Radio is tough. The relationship you have with your audience is more intimate than with any other. It's just you and them. If your story's wonky they'll sniff it out and switch off.

AL SMITH IS A TELEVISION AND RADIO SCRIPTWRITER.

DRAMATIC LANGUAGE

The most important tools a writer of radio drama has are the **words** that they choose. With a well-chosen sentence a writer can create an instant picture in a listener's mind.

Dramatists think carefully about the associations that different words have, choosing ones that evoke the atmosphere they want to create. The rhythm of language can be important too in creating a specific mood.

Reading dialogue aloud can help you to think about the pace of a scene.

CHARACTERS AND CONFLICT

Just like every other kind of story, a radio play is about characters and conflict. Radio drama works best when there are only a few characters in a scene, unlike in films and TV shows, so dramatists limit the dialogue to two or three characters so that it's easier for listeners to keep track of who is speaking.

Make the voices of your characters distinctive – in both what they say and how they say it. Dialogue should show the conflict at the heart of every scene, with words fuelled by the emotions that are being explored.

MIKE WALKER SAYS ...

With radio you really do have a theatre as large as the universe in that sense. You're using the muscle of the listener's imagination — they're doing the work with you.

MIKE WALKER IS A RADIO DRAMATIST.

JULIE MAYHEW SAYS ...

I find radio writing is closer to novel writing than it is to writing for the theatre. This is because in both the novel and the radio play I tend to explore the characters' internal worlds, as well as the action. By that I mean, I write what the characters are doing, but also what they're thinking — and often how there is a clash between these two things.

JULIE MAYHEW IS AN AUTHOR AND RADIO PLAYWRIGHT.

SOUND EFFECTS

There are no visual images to guide a listener, so writers of radio drama use sound effects to evoke different settings. From blaring car horns to show a driver stuck in roadworks to the sound of horses' hooves as Sherlock Holmes chases Professor Moriarty, the time and place of the story can be suggested through sound.

A change of sound effect can signal a shift of scene, helping the listener to get a sense of place before a character even begins to speak.

Remember that you're writing for radio. The sight of a sky filled with alien spaceships hovering over the Houses of Parliament would need to be expressed by characters' voicing their fear of what they can see, running away, and with dramatic sound effects.

WRITING FOR VIDEOGAMES

New technology has created new opportunities for writers to tell stories. Videogaming is a multi-billion pound industry that brings together designers, artists, programmers and software engineers, but at the heart of every game is a story.

GAMING GENRES

Just like books, films and TV shows, videogames come in many genres. From first-person shooters to role-playing games, open-world adventures to simulation and strategy games, the kinds of stories a writer can tell in a videogame are influenced by how the game will be played.

In some videogames the player is at the heart of the action, experiencing the game world through the avatar that they control. In other games such as *Civilization*, the player has godlike powers, controlling the game world and the lives of the virtual people who populate it.

What genre of game would your story fit best?

Remember some videogames can combine more than one genre.

CUT SCENES AND CHARACTERS

From treasure hunter Nathan Drake in the adventure game *Uncharted* to strange science fiction heroes Ratchet and Clank, videogames are filled with unforgettable characters. In a novel a reader can identify with the lead character but in a videogame they actually become them. This means that videogame writers need to create characters with player appeal. Think up distinctive and diverse characters to populate your game. They need to reflect the different people who might choose to play it.

When scripting a videogame, a writer can introduce characters through 'cut scenes'. These mini-films can set up **situations, new environments** and **hazards** the player must respond to and explore as they move through the game world.

GAMEPLAY AND GOALS

In every videogame there are goals that a player needs to achieve. These might be hidden pieces of treasure to find or a puzzle that they have to solve. As the game is played, the story then branches in different ways depending on the decisions the player makes. What are the goals that will drive the story in the videogame you are writing?

A videogame writer needs to carefully consider the choices they offer the player in the game.

What consequences could different actions have?

Game designers often build in rewards at different points in a game, such as equipment that can be unlocked by the player's achievements. You could create a plan showing the different paths a player might follow in each section of the game.

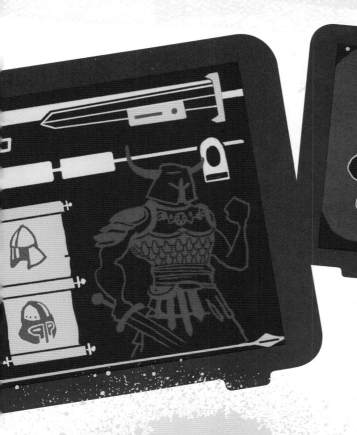

LEVEL UP

Game designers want people to pick up a controller and quickly learn what they are supposed to do. The beginning stages of a game should set a player easier challenges than they'll face later in the game. This allows a player to improve their skills and build up their experience before they take on more difficult goals.

When planning a videogame, think about it as a sequence of situations and challenges with each one being slightly more difficult than the last.

Talk to your friends about the videogames and find out which parts they like the most. Can you put any of these elements into your videogame script?

RHIANNA PRATCHETT SAYS ...

Story is important, but games are gameplay-led, mechanics-led. The story has to find a way to work within that. Ideally the story should fold into gameplay and level design in a way that feels seamless, rather than, 'Oh, here's the game and here's a story sitting on top of it'.

RHIANNA PRATCHETT IS A SCRIPTWRITER WHO HAS WORKED ON VIDEOGAMES SUCH AS **TOMB RAIDER**, **HEAVENLY SWORD** AND **MIRROR'S EDGE**.

153

WRITING  FICTION

If you've ever fallen in love with a fictional world or reached the end of a book and not wanted to say goodbye to the characters inside its pages, you might find yourself tempted to write fan fiction. Fan fiction takes characters and worlds that other authors have created and weaves new stories using these.

OMG!!!!

OMG!!!!

OMG!!!!

SHARING STORIES

Writers of fan fiction often share their stories on story apps like Wattpad or fan fiction websites. In these online spaces there are millions of readers who are eager to hear more about their favourite books, films and TV shows.

Fan fiction authors can post up their own stories featuring established characters such as Sherlock Holmes and find a ready-made audience. Some story apps and websites allow readers to subscribe to an author's story so they get alerts when new chapters are released. This helps **create a buzz** and some authors find their story has **thousands of fans** by the time the last chapter is uploaded.

'The whole point of fanfiction is that you get to play inside somebody else's universe. Rewrite the rules. Or bend them. The story doesn't have to end. You can stay in this world, this world you love, as long as you want, as long as you keep thinking of new stories.'
FANGIRL by Rainbow Rowell

REMIX A BOOK

You can retell   character's perspective or imagine what might have happened if a key moment was changed.

Stephanie Meyer reimagined her own Twilight novel by swapping the genders of the two lead characters to create a new book entitled *Life and Death*.

You can also take characters from different books to create new stories. Comic books are big fans of this technique mashing together superheroes from different universes in huge crossover events. In these stories you can find Judge Dredd arresting Batman and discover who would win a fight between Superman and the Hulk.

NEIL GAIMAN SAYS ...

I think that playing with other people's ideas and work is a perfectly valid way to make art. I also think it's much wiser and safer to do it with ideas and work that are comfortably in the public domain if you want your work to be seen professionally.

NEIL GAIMAN IS AN AUTHOR OF ADULT AND CHILDREN'S FICTION.

COPYRIGHTS AND WRONGS

When creating fan fiction you need to be careful. The author of the original book that you have borrowed a character from owns the copyright in their creation. Some writers don't mind their fans creating stories set in their fictional worlds, but you shouldn't try to publish these.

Books go out of copyright a number of years after the author who wrote them has died. It varies from country to country so you will need to check your copyright laws. In the UK, you could publish a story featuring Dracula whose author, Bram Stoker, died in 1912, but you wouldn't be able to include any characters from today's bestseller lists.

BLAM

INDEX

ACKNOWLEDGEMENTS

We are grateful for permission from the following authors to use their words from the sources indicated:

Malorie Blackman c/o The Agency (London) Ltd, on www.malorieblackman.co.uk, © Malorie Blackman; **Don Calame** and Guardian News & Media Ltd, in *The Guardian*, March 2012; **Alex Campbell** c/o David Godwin Associates, and Guardian News & Media Ltd, in *The Guardian*, November 2014; **Lucinda Coxon** c/o The Agency (London) Ltd, and Guardian News & Media Ltd, in *The Guardian*, September 2008; © Lucinda Coxon 2008; **Joe Craig** on www.turkeyonthehill.blogspot.co.uk, April 2014; and Guardian News & Media Ltd, in *The Guardian*, November 2015; **Natasha Desborough** c/o MBA Literary, and Guardian News & Media Ltd, in *The Guardian*, March 2015; **Chris D'Lacey** c/o Johnson & Alcock Ltd, and Guardian News & Media Ltd, in *The Guardian*, June 2016; **Neil Gaiman** c/o Writers House, from 'Where do you get your ideas?' on www.neilgaiman.com, and from 'Neil Gaiman's opinion on fan fiction' on Tumblr; Guardian News & Media Ltd, in *The Guardian*, August 2011; **Mark Haddon** c/o Aitken Alexander Associates, and Powells Books, from an interview on Powells.com, 24 June 2003; **Alwyn Hamilton** c/o The Bent Agency, and Guardian News & Media Ltd, in *The Guardian*, March 2016; **Frances Hardinge**, © Frances Hardinge 2016, interviewed in *Writing* magazine, www.writers-online.co.uk, May 2016; **M John Harrison** c/o Mic Cheetham Associates, in *Fantastic Metropolis*, 2001; **Jane Lawes** and Bloomsbury Publishing plc, from Writersandartists.co.uk; **Caroline Lawrence** c/o Eddison Pearson Literary Agency, and Guardian News & Media Ltd, in *The Guardian*, March 2012; **Ursula Le Guin** c/o MBA Literary, interviewed by John Wray in *The Paris Review*, 2013; **Estelle Maskame** c/o Black & White Publishing Ltd, and Guardian News & Media Ltd, in *The Guardian*, June 2015; **Julie Mayhew** c/o LBA Books, interviewed for The Reading Agency; **Shane Meadows** c/o Casarotto Ramsay & Associates, interviewed for Film4, www.film4.com; **Michael Morpurgo** c/o David Higham Associates, on Readingzone.com; **Patrick Ness** c/o Michelle Kass Associates, and Independent Media, from 'On another planet' by Daniel Hahn in *The Independent*, May 2010; **Jeff Norton** from 'Word Building', March 2014, www.jeffnorton.com; **James Patterson** c/o Williams & Connolly LLP, interviewed in *Writer's Digest*, 2009; **Bryony Pearce** in an interview c 2010; **Rhianna Pratchett** from 'Rhianna Pratchett paves a new way for female heroes' by Dean Takashi, www.venturebeat.com, February 2016; **Philip Pullman** c/o A P Watt at United Agents, on www.goodreads.com; **Chris Riddell** c/o LAW, and The Telegraph Media Group, interviewed in *The Telegraph*, November 2011; **Michele Roberts** c/o Aitken Alexander Associates Ltd, on Booktrust website; **J K Rowling** c/o The Blair Partnership, on Scholastic author page, www.scholastic.com; **Lance Rubin** and Guardian News & Media Ltd, in *The Guardian*, January 2016; **Angie Sage** and Guardian News & Media Ltd, in *The Guardian*, November 2015; **Al Smith** c/o United Agents, and the BBC, 'Writing for Radio: Find Your "Itch"', *Writersroom*, www.bbc.co.uk, August 2014; **Maggie Stiefvater** c/o Andrea Brown Literary Agency, and New York Media, from 'Maggie Stiefvater says YA is a bullshit label' by Claire Landsbaum, www.vulture.com, April 2016; **Laini Taylor** c/o Eyebait Management Inc, from an interview, and from '5 Writing Tips', *Publishers Weekly*, November 2012; **Sally Wainright** c/o The Agency, interviewed in *Writing* magazine, and the BBC; **Mike Walker** c/o David Higham Associates, and the BBC, on www.bbc.co.uk/worldservice; **Jon Walter** c/o Mulcahy Associates, and Guardian News & Media Ltd, in *The Guardian*, August 2014.

We are also grateful for permission to include extracts from the following copyright work:

M T Anderson: *Feed* (Candlewick, 2003), © M T Anderson 2002, reprinted by permission of Walker Books Ltd, London SE11 5HJ, www.walker.co.uk. **Faye Bird**: *My Second Life* (Usborne, 2014), © Faye Bird 2014, reprinted by permission of the publishers, Usborne Publishing, 83-85 Saffron Hill, London EC1N 8RT, www.usborne.com, and Farrar, Straus & Giroux LLC, Macmillan Children's Publishing Group. All rights reserved. **Sita Brahmachari**: *Artichoke Hearts* (Macmillan Children's Books, 2011), © Sita Brahmachari 2011, reprinted by permission of MBA Literary on behalf of the author. **Dan Brown**: *The Lost Symbol* (Corgi, 2010), © Dan Brown 2009, 2010, reprinted by permission of the publishers, The Random House Group Ltd, and Doubleday, an imprint of Knopf Doubleday Publishing Group, a division of Penguin Random House LLC. All rights reserved. **Natasha Carthew**: *Winter Damage* (Bloomsbury, 2013), © Natasha Carthew 2012, reprinted by permission of Bloomsbury Publishing Plc. **H M Castor**: *VIII* (Templar, 2011), © H M Castor 2010, reprinted by permission of the publishers. **Suzanne Collins**: *The Hunger Games* (Scholastic, 2008) © Suzanne Collins 2008, reprinted by permission of Scholastic Inc. **Anne-Marie Conway**: *Butterfly Summer* (Usborne, 2012), © Anne-Marie Conway 2012, reprinted by permission Usborne Publishing, 83-85 Saffron Hill, London EC1N 8RT, www.usborne.com, and A M Heath & Co Ltd for the author. **Dave Cousins**: *15 Days without a Head* (OUP, 2012), © Dave Cousins 2012, reprinted by permission of the author c/o the Sarah Manson Literary Agency. **Sara Crowe**: *Bone Jack* (Anderson Press, 2014), reprinted by permission of the publishers and of the author c/o Hardman & Swainson Literary Agency. **James Dashner**: *The Maze Runner* (Chicken House, 2010), © James Dashner 2010, reprinted by permission of Chicken House Ltd. All rights reserved. **Gerald Durrell**: *My Family and Other Animals* (Puffin, 2016), © The Estate of Gerald Durrell 1955, reprinted by permission of Curtis Brown Group Ltd, London on behalf of the Estate of Gerald Durrell. **Christopher Edge**: *The Black Crow Conspiracy* (Nosy Crow, 2014), reprinted by permission of the author and the publisher; *Twelve Minutes to Midnight* (Pearson, 2013), reprinted by permission of the author. **Tom Ellen** and **Lucy Ivison**: *Never Evers* (Chicken House, 2016), © Tom Ellen and Lucy Ivison 2016, reprinted by permission of Chicken House Ltd. All rights reserved. **Clare Furniss**: *The Year of the Rat* (Simon & Schuster, 2014), © Clare Furniss 2014, reprinted by permission of Simon & Schuster UK. **Neil Gaiman**: *The Graveyard Book* (Bloomsbury, 2008), © Neil Gaiman 2008, reprinted by permission of Bloomsbury Publishing Plc and HarperCollins Publishers, USA. **Sally Gardner**: *Maggot Moon* (Hot Key Books, 2013), © Sally Gardner 2012, reprinted by permission of the publishers, Bonnier Zaffre Ltd, and Candlewick Press. **Alan Gibbons**: *Hate* (Indigo, 2014), © Alan Gibbon 2014, reprinted by permission of the publishers, Orion Cxhildren's Books, an imprint of Hachette Children's Books, London. **Keith Gray**: *The Return of Johnny Kemp* (Barrington Stoke, 2014), © Keith Gray 2009, reprinted by permission of Barrington Stoke Ltd; *Ostrich Boys* (Bodley Head, 2008), © Keith Gray 2008, reprinted by permission of the publishers, The Random House Group Ltd and Random House Children's Books, a division of Penguin Random House LLC. All rights reserved. **John Green**: *Paper Towns* (Bloomsbury, 2010), © John Green 2008, reprinted by permission of the publishers, Bloomsbury Publishing Plc, and Dutton Children's Books, an imprint of Penguin Young Readers Group, a division of Penguin Random House LLC; *An Abundance of Katherines* (Puffin, 2012), © John Green 2006, and *The Fault in our Stars* (Penguin, 2012), © John Green 2012, reprinted by permission of the publishers, Penguin Books Ltd and Dutton Children's Books, an imprint of Penguin Young Readers Group, a division of Penguin Random House LLC. **Mark Haddon**: *The Curious Incident of the Dog in the Night Time: A novel* (Cape, 2003), © Mark Haddon 2003, reprinted by permission of the publishers, The Random House Group Ltd and Doubleday, an imprint of Knopf Doubleday Publishing Group, a division of Penguin Random House LLC. All rights reserved. **Frances Hardinge**: *Fly By Night* (Macmillan Children's Books, 2005), © Frances Hardinge 2005, reprinted by permission of Macmillan Children's Books, an imprint of Pan Macmillan, a division of Macmillan Publishers International Ltd. **Sam Hepburn**: *Chasing the Dark* (Chicken House, 2013), © Sam Hepburn 2013, reprinted by permission of Chicken House Ltd. All rights reserved. **S E Hinton**: *The Outsiders* (Penguin, 2007), © S E Hinton 1967, renewed 1995, reprinted by permission of the publishers, Penguin Books Ltd and Viking Children's Books, an imprint of Penguin Young Readers Group, a division of Penguin Random House LLC. **Cathy Hopkins**: *Million Dollar Mates* (Simon & Schuster, 2010), © Cathy Hopkins 2010, reprinted by permission of Simon & Schuster UK. **Nick Hornby**: *The Complete Polysyllabic Spree* (Penguin, 2015), © Nick Hornby 2006, reprinted by permission of Penguin Books Ltd and the author c/o Rogers, Coleridge & White Ltd, 20 Powis Mews, London W11 1JN. **Anthony Horowitz**: *Point Blanc* (Walker, 2015), © Stormbreaker Productions Ltd 2001, reprinted by permission of Walker Books Ltd, London SE11 5HJ, www.walker.co.uk, and Curtis Brown Group Ltd London on behalf of Anthony Horowitz. **Stephen King**: *On Writing: A Memoir of the Craft* (Hodder, 2012), reprinted by permission of Hodder & Stoughton Ltd. **Ursula K Le Guin**: *A Wizard of Earthsea* (Penguin, 2012), © 1968, 1996 by The Inter-Vivos Trust for the Le Guin Children, reprinted by permission of MBA Literary on behalf of the author, and Houghton Mifflin Harcourt Publishing Company. All rights reserved. **Geraldine McCaughrean**: *The Middle of Nowhere* (Usborne, 2014), © Geraldine McCaughrean 2014, reprinted by permission of David Higham Associates. **Anthony McGowan**: *Hello Darkness* (Walker, 2013), © Anthony McGowan 2013, reprinted by permission of Walker Books Ltd, London SE11 5HJ, www.walker.co.uk, and of the author c/o Kinsford Campbell Literary Agents. **Patrick Ness**: *The Knife of Never Letting Go* (Walker, 2014), © Patrick Ness 2008, reprinted by permission of Walker Books Ltd, London SE11 5HJ, www.walker.co.uk. **Lauren Oliver**: *Before I Fall* (Hodder & Stoughton, 2010), Laura Schlechter 2010, reprinted by permission of Hodder & Stoughton Ltd and Inkwell Management LLC on behalf of the author. **George Orwell**: *Nineteen Eighty-Four* (Penguin, 2013), © George Orwell 1949, reprinted by permission of Bill Hamilton as the Literary Executor of the Estate of the late Sonia Brownell Orwell c/o A M Heath & Co Ltd. **Philip Pullman**: *Northern Lights* (Scholastic, 2015), © Philip Pullman 1995, reprinted by permission of Scholastic Ltd. **Terry Pratchett**: *Johnny and the Dead* (Corgi, 2005/HarperCollins 2006), copyright © Terry Pratchett 1993, reprinted by permission of The Random House Group Ltd, and Colin Smythe Ltd. **Michael Punke**: *The Revenant: A novel of revenge* (The Borough Press, 2015), © Michael Punke 2015, reprinted by permission of the publishers, HarperCollins Publishers Ltd and St Martin's Press. All rights reserved. **Philip Reeve**: *Mortal Engines* (Scholastic, 2002), © Philip Reeve 2002, reprinted by permission of Scholastic Ltd. **Ransom Riggs**: *Miss Peregrine's Home for Peculiar Children* (Headline, 2013), ©Ransom Riggs 2011, 2013, reprinted by permission of the publishers, Headline Publishing Group and Quirk Books, Philadelphia. **James Riordan**: *The Prisoner* (OUP, 2004), © James Riordan 1995, reprinted by permission of Oxford University Press. **Rainbow Rowell**: *Fangirl* (Macmillan, 2014), © Rainbow Rowell 2014, reprinted by permission of Macmillan Children's Books, an imprint of Pan Macmillan, a division of Macmillan Publishers International Ltd; *Eleanor and Park* (Orion, 2012), © Rainbow Rowell 2012, reprinted by permission of the publishers, The Orion Publishing Group and St Martin's Press. All rights reserved. **Katharine Rundell**: *Rooftoppers* (Faber, 2013), © Katharine Rundell, 2013, reprinted by permission of the publishers, Faber & Faber Ltd and Simon & Schuster Books for Young Readers, an imprint of Simon & Schuster Children's Publishing Division. All rights reserved. **Tess Sharpe**: *Far From You* (Indigo, 2014), © Tess Sharpe 2014, reprinted by permission of the publishers, Orion Children's Books, an imprint of Hachette Children's Books, London. **Dave Shelton**: *Thirteen Chairs* (David Fickling, 2014), © Dave Shelton 2014, reprinted by permission of David Fickling Books. **Holly Smale**: *All That Glitters* (HarperCollins Childrens, 2015), © Holly Smale 2015, reprinted by permission of HarperCollins Publishers Ltd. **Dodie Smith**: *I Capture the Castle* (Penguin, 2016), © Dodie Smith 1948, reprinted by permission of Laurence Fitch Ltd. **Lemony Snicket**: *When Did You See Her Last?* (Egmont, 2013), © Lemony Snicket 2013, reprinted by permission of the publishers, Egmont UK Ltd, Little, Brown Books for Young Readers, and HarperCollins Publishers, Canada. **William Sutcliffe**: *The Wall* (Bloomsbury, 2014), © William Sutcliffe 2014, reprinted by permission of Bloomsbury Publishing Plc. **Donna Tartt**: *The Secret History* (Penguin Red Classic, 2006), © Donna Tartt 1992, reprinted by permission of the publishers, Penguin Books Ltd and Alfred A Knopf, an imprint of the Knopf Doubleday Publishing Group, a division of Penguin Random House LLC. **J.R.R. Tolkien**: *The Lord of the Rings*, Volume 1: *The Fellowship of the Ring* (HarperCollins, 2013), and Volume 3: *Return of the King* (HarperCollins, 2012); © J.R.R.Tolkien 1966; letter 131, *The Letters of J R R Tolkien* edited by Humphrey Carpenter with the assistance of Christopher Tolkien (Allen & Unwin, 1981), reprinted by permission of HarperCollins Publishers Ltd. **Sue Townsend**: *The Secret Diary of Adrian Mole, Aged 13¾* (Penguin, 2014), © Sue Townsend 1982, reprinted by permission of the publishers, The Random House Group Ltd, HarperCollins Publishers, USA, and of Curtis Brown Group Ltd, London on behalf of Sue Townsend. **Jon Walter**: *My Name's Not Friday* (David Fickling, 2015), © Jon Walter 2015, reprinted by permission of David Fickling Books. **Scott Westerfeld**: *Uglies* (Simon & Schuster, 2010), ©Scott Westerfeld 2006, reprinted by permission of Simon & Schuster UK.